Peter Dickinson's

The Kin

SUTH'S STORY

Peter Dickinson's
The Kin
SUTH'S STORY

GROSSET & DUNLAP • NEW YORK

Library of Congress Cataloging-in-Publication Data
Dickinson, Peter, 1927-
[Suth's story]
Peter Dickinson's Suth's story / [cover art by Nenad Jakesevic].
p.   cm — (The Kin)
Summary: When cut off from their kin and lost in the desert
200,000 years ago, Suth and five other orphans struggle to survive
and to find their way to safety.
[1. Prehistoric peoples—Fiction.   2. Survival—Fiction.
3. Orphans—Fiction.]   I. Title.   II. Series: Dickinson, Peter, 1927-
Kin.
PZ7.D562Pg   1998   [Fic]—dc21   98-14226   CIP   AC

ISBN 0-448-41709-X
B C D E F G H I J

For Nicholas

Peter Dickinson's
The Kin

SUTH'S STORY

About two hundred thousand years ago, on a hot continent, the first true, modern human beings evolved. Some experts believe that what made them different from earlier humans was that they had language. They could speak.

The new humans did well and their numbers grew, so they moved outward from the area where they began. This happened in waves, with long intervals between. My story is about a group of these new humans, the Kin, just after a fresh movement of people has driven them from the lands where they have lived for as long as they can remember.

I have made almost all of it up. The real people who lived in those days left very few traces—the stone tools they made, fossils of their own bones and the bones of animals they ate, the ashes of their fires, and so on. What were they like? How did they live? Even the experts can only guess, using their imaginations and the few facts they do know. So that's what I've done too.

This is the first of four stories of the Kin. It is the story of a boy called Suth.

I have put "Oldtales" between the chapters. I believe that we have always wondered how we came to be here, and why things happen, and whether there is somebody wise and strong and strange who made everything in the first place. One of the ways we wonder is to invent stories. The Oldtales are the stories Suth's people have made up, to explain things to themselves.

—Peter Dickinson

1

Fingers pressed Suth's cheek, in the corner by the jawbone. He woke. A mouth breathed in his ear.

"Come."

Noli.

She withdrew.

Carefully, as if merely turning in his sleep, he rolled himself away from the rest of the Kin, who slept in a huddle for warmth from the desert night. Suth was a child, and now had no father or mother, so his place was on the outside of the huddle. So was Noli's, for the same reasons.

He lay still, waited, rolled again and on hands and knees crawled silently clear. There was a half moon rising, casting long shadows.

"Here." Noli's faint whisper came from the blackness beside a boulder. Suth crawled toward her. She took his hand, put her other hand to his mouth for silence, and led him away.

In the shadow of another boulder she stopped and put her mouth to his ear.

"I dreamed. Moonhawk came. She showed me water."

"Where?"

She pointed back, almost along the line they had traveled all day.

"In the morning you tell Bal," whispered Suth.

"He says I lie."

She was right. Bal was their leader. He dreamed the dreams that Moonhawk sent, showing him things he needed to know for the safety of the Kin. But then it had been Noli who had dreamed about the coming of the murderous strangers, who did not belong to any of the Kins, and spoke with words that none of them knew. It had been Noli who had dreamed of the killing of fathers and brothers, the taking of mothers and sisters.

Moonhawk had not shown these things to Bal, and when Noli had told of them he had struck her and said that she lied. Moonhawk came only to him in his dreams.

And yet Noli's dream had come true, and what was left of the Kin had fled from the Good Places they knew, and Bal had led them into Dry Hills, looking for somewhere new to live.

Then again Noli had dreamed. In this dream Moonhawk had come to her and shown her the endless desert, waterless and foodless, that they would come to after they passed Dry Hills. And again, when she had told her dream, Bal had struck her and said that she lied.

And yet it had come true.

"In the morning we tell the others," said Suth.

"No, we go alone. We go now, along the way we came. We find the little ones that were left behind. We take them to the water. All this Moonhawk showed me."

She took him by the hand and led him on. He didn't resist, though for the first time in his life he was leaving the Kin. He was walking away into the night without any adult to lead him, with only a girl for company, even younger than himself. Ever since the fight with the strangers, when he had seen his father killed and his mother taken, he had been in a kind of dull dream. Nothing made sense anymore. Moonhawk told Noli what to do, and Noli told Suth. That was enough.

They found their way without trouble. They were used to wide empty spaces, and their sense of direction was strong. Here and there they remembered the shape of a boulder, or a dry ravine, that they had passed on the outward journey. And the night dews freshened the faint scents that the Kin had left as they had come this way. There were no other smells to confuse them. Nothing lived here. In all the long day they had seen no tracks, nothing that moved, not a lizard, not even a scorpion. At least where there was nothing to eat there would be no big hunters stalking the night.

They walked at the steady pace that the Kin had used, journeying between one Good Place and the next. It grew colder.

Slowly the moon rose. When it was almost halfway up the sky they stopped, without a word from either of them. They raised their heads and sniffed. Water.

"Moonhawk showed you this?" said Suth.

"No, not this. She showed me water in the hills."

"Why did we not smell this when we came by in the daytime? Why did Bal not smell it? He finds water where no one else can find it."

"I do not know. Is it a dew trap, Suth? Like the dew trap at Tarutu Rock?"

They turned and in a short while came to a wide pit in the ground. As they walked down into it, they felt new layers of chill gathering around them. Soon the rocks they trod on were slippery with dew. But this was not like the dew trap they knew, where the moisture gathered at the bottom into a rocky pool, which didn't dry up until the sun was high. Here there was only a gravel floor and the water seeped away. They kneeled and licked the wetness from a large sloping boulder. It was not enough to swallow, but soothed their sore lips and parched mouths. For a little while they rested and licked and rested, then found their way back to their trail and walked on.

By the time that the moon was overhead they could see, out across the desert plain, the barrier of jagged hills through which Bal had led them two days earlier. Suth remembered how they had stopped on the last ridge and stared at what lay before them under the evening sun, a vast flatness, mottled yellow and gray, boulders and pebbles and ash and sand, and not a leaf or stem anywhere, all still pulsing with heat after the burning day.

Some of the Kin had begun to mutter unhappily. Bal had swung and glared at them, hunching his shoulders and shaking his mane out to show them who was leader.

"There are new Good Places there," he had growled. "Water and game. Moonhawk showed me. Moonhawk showed me this too. We must go fast through the desert, or we die. We must carry our small ones. But they are too many. Some have no fathers, no mothers, to carry them. Those we leave here. We build a lair for them. In the lair they have shade. They are safe from animals. We find our new Good Places. Then some of us come back. They fetch these small ones. Perhaps they still live."

He had chosen four children who had lost their parents in the fighting—Po and Mana, who were too little to walk all day, Tinu, who was older but weak from a fever, and Noli's little brother, Otan, who could stand but not yet walk. The others had helped Noli carry him this far.

Nobody had argued, though they knew that the children would live for only a day, and perhaps a night, but not another day. They could see that what Bal said was true. The Good Places he promised them might or might not exist, but if they tried to carry these extra children through the dreadful desert below they would never get there.

So the next morning they had found a place where one rock leaned against another to make a kind of cave and had put the children into it. They walled them in with smaller rocks to keep them safe from animals, and told them to wait there, and left them looking scared and dazed. Noli had let them take Otan from her, and then turned away, weeping. But she'd said nothing.

"They are dead," Suth said.

"No," said Noli.

They walked on. Now the moon moved down the sky. Day would come before it set. Slowly the hills loomed nearer and higher and they began to climb. As they did the moonlight paled and the shadows lost their sharpness. Day came almost at once, a clear gray light still fresh with the night chill and the dew. To their right the sky turned pale gold. Every detail of the dry and rocky slope stood sharp and clear.

Noli looked ahead and pointed. There were the two leaning rocks. This was the place.

She quickened her pace, but Suth caught her wrist. Something had moved, a blue gray shape like a shadow prowling in front of the two rocks. It returned, nosing at the piled stones, sniffing for the flesh behind them. It scratched at the pile with a paw. Some kind of fox-thing, though different from the yellow and brown foxes that had scavenged around the Good Places that the Kin had been driven from.

Suth picked up a rock, weighed it in his hand, put it soundlessly down and chose a heavier one. Noli took another. Side by side but a little apart the two crept forward, moving and pausing and moving as they had watched their elders do, hunting unsuspecting prey. The foxes that Suth knew had learned to be afraid of people, and were shy and quick and hard to catch, but this one was too excited by the smells from behind the rock pile to notice as the hunters crept nearer.

Not until Suth was only two paces away did it sense something, turn and see him. It was not just in color that it was different. It did not fear people.

Snarling, it leaped for Suth's belly, but his arm was already poised for a blow. He swung as it came, and the rock caught the fox full force on the head, knocking it sideways. Then Noli was on it, pounding down with her rock. It thrashed aside and tried to rise, but before it was on its feet Suth struck it again with all his strength at the point where the neck joined the skull. It collapsed, twitched once, and lay still.

They struck it several more blows to

make sure, then left it lying and went to the rock pile. There was no sound from inside.

They are dead, Suth thought.

"Are you there, Tinu?" he said softly. "Mana? Po? It is me, Suth. And Noli."

A faint mumbling sound answered. That was Tinu, who had a twisted mouth and did not speak clearly. There was a wail from a smaller child. With a gush of hope Suth started to pull the pile of rocks down. As soon as she could reach, Noli joined in. The sun rose on their backs. When the wall was low enough they craned over.

Tinu was crouching in the little cave with Otan in her arms. Po sat huddled beside her, blinking at the light. Mana lay on her side, unmoving, but she stirred and moaned as Suth reached in, took Otan, and passed him to Noli. He pulled more rocks down until Tinu could help Po and Mana, still half asleep, to scramble out. Tinu came last.

Noli was cradling little Otan to her chest, feeling for his heartbeat and listening for his breath. "My brother lives," she whispered, shuddering with relief.

The others waited. Three pairs of dark,

anxious eyes gazed at Suth. He could see what they were thinking. *Where was the rest of the Kin? Where were the grown men and women? Where was Bal, the leader?* Po and Mana were little more than babies, though Po was sturdy and big for his age. Suth had never taken much notice of Mana, a quiet, watchful little girl, with the same dark skin and black, coarse hair as everyone else in the eight Kins.

Tinu was different. Something had been wrong with her mouth when she was born, so that her jaw opened more sideways than down and she never learned to speak properly. She was small too, for her age, and extremely skinny, with insect-thin limbs. She hated to be noticed and looked at. As soon as Suth's glance fell on her, she turned her head away.

"Thirsty," she mumbled.

"Noli knows where water is," said Suth.

"It is not far," said Noli. "Suth killed food. You come."

Suth heaved the dead fox onto his shoulder. Noli settled Otan onto her hip and led the way, with Tinu next and the two small ones scrambling behind her across the stony slope. Suth came last, helping them when they needed him. He felt different now. The fox was heavy, but its weight gave him strength. He had done something. He had killed food. These others, they needed him. Without him, they would die.

Oldtale

The First Good Place

Black Antelope was chief among the First Ones.

He said, "Now we make a place where we can live."

He breathed upon the bare ground, and where he had breathed the young grass grew, tender for him to eat.

Then Snake crawled through the grasslands, making tracks, which he could follow. And Crocodile dug holes and filled them with clean water, where she could lie and wait. And Weaver planted trees, so that his wives had somewhere to hang their nests, and Parrot added sweet nuts and fruits to the trees, because he was greedy, and the Ant Mother chewed the fallen branches from the trees and mixed the chewings into the ground to make good soft earth for her nests, and Fat Pig planted the earth with juicy roots to fill his stomach, and Moonhawk built crags from which she could watch while the others slept, and Little Bat made caves in the crags, where she could hide from Moonhawk.

So they all worked together to make the First Good Place, according to their needs.

Only Monkey did nothing.

He watched the others at work, and then he climbed Weaver's trees and ate Parrot's fruits and nuts, and he dug in the Ant Mother's earth and ate Fat Pig's roots, and he slept in Little Bat's caves and drank from Crocodile's water holes, and he set traps in Snake's tracks, and scrambled over Moonhawk's crags. But he did not often go into Black Antelope's grasslands because he was the strongest and Monkey was afraid of him.

2

The water was a thin trickle, oozing down a narrow crack in the cliff. They couldn't get their faces in to lap, so all they could do was slide a hand and wet their fingertips and suck. The water had a strong taste and a faint smell of foul eggs, like the water at Yellowhole, where the Kin used to drink. Before she had any herself, Noli gave her fingers to Otan to suck. At first nothing happened, but then the small dry lips moved faintly, and a hand clenched and unclenched. It was the first sign of life that anyone but Noli had seen in him.

After a while, Tinu found that if she put her fingers into the crack at a certain angle the water ran along the lower edge of her palm and gathered into drops on her wrist bone, where she could suck them off before they fell. The others copied her.

As soon as he'd drunk enough, Suth looked for the right sort of rock, so that he could try to make a cutter and butcher little pieces of meat off the fox carcass for the small ones to chew. He had often watched his father stoneworking, and had tried to copy what he did, but it was men's work. Boys didn't get taught it. His father had known which were the right rocks, and where to strike them, but he couldn't say how he knew. His eye and his hand had told him *this one* and *here*. So all Suth had been able to do was watch, and then try for himself. What he'd learned was that it wasn't as easy as it looked.

Besides, good rocks were only found in some places. There might be none on this hillside at all. Suth chose several and squatted down by a flat boulder. Steadying one rock on it, he hammered down with another, using a slanting blow, trying to chip off a large flake.

Nothing happened. He tried again and again, but the target rock kept twisting in his grasp. Between their turns at the water the others watched him, as he tried different rocks and different angles of strike. Sometimes he broke off a few chips, but nothing large enough to grasp and nothing with a cutting edge to it.

Without warning the rock he had been using as a hammer shattered as it struck the target. The pieces flew apart. The shock numbed his arm to the elbow. He was rubbing the feeling back into it when Tinu, always shy and uncertain, anxiously showed him a flake that had fallen at her feet, a round sliver so thin in places that when he held it up he could see light through it. Testing it with his thumb, he found that along one edge it was as sharp as anything he had seen his father make, though he knew his father would have thrown it away because it was so fragile. A good cutter was thicker than this, but he thought it might do if he was careful. He laughed at the luck of it, and the small ones laughed too, not understanding why.

Thirsty again after the work he went back to the crack. While he was slowly drinking,

Tinu came up holding a stick she had broken from one of the scrawny bushes that grew in the gully below. These were the first plants Suth had seen in three days.

Tinu waited till he had finished, and then edged up, as if she was expecting him to bark at her to go away, and eased the end of the stick into the crack. Suth watched her, puzzled, as she tried it at different angles. Then, wonderfully, a drop of water appeared on a side twig beneath it, and another and another. She cupped her free hand under them and caught them as they fell, until her palm was full. She lapped the water up and looked at him, still as if she expected him to yell at her or strike her.

"Good, good," he said, smiling. "Now you show Noli."

While the others were learning how to use the stick, he picked up the fox and laid it on its back. Holding the flake of rock between thumb and forefinger he drew the cutting edge slowly along the seam of the belly, again and again, never pressing hard for fear of breaking his cutter but gradually slicing through the tough skin.

The three girls watched in silence, but Po squatted by his side, jaw set, frowning, longing to join in, longing to help. Suth was about to snarl at him to keep clear when he thought, *Po saw his father die. He saw his mother taken. He was walled in a dark place for a day and a night. He does not understand any of this. He does not understand there is no Kin now for him to belong to. I understand all this. With Noli's help I am leader now. We are their father and their mother.*

So he told Po to hold the fox's tail clear while he worked. It didn't need holding, but it gave Po something to do, and they both felt better.

Slowly a scratch formed. The scratch became a cut, and then Suth was slicing into the fat beneath the skin. He sawed at the ends of the cut, widening it until he could plunge his hand through and pull out the guts. Still very careful of his precious tool he cut the liver free.

Suth was the leader now, so he ate first, cutting himself a mouthful before hacking off pieces for the others while he chewed. Fox meat was better roasted, and even then had a strong, rancid taste. Still, it was food, and none of them had eaten cooked food since the fight, when the strangers had taken away their fire log along with the women.

They chewed in silence. Noli put her mouth to Otan's and forced some of her chewings between his lips. He sucked them in and gaped for more.

"That is enough," said Suth, when they had eaten the liver and the heart, though his own stomach still ached with hunger.

"Yes," said Noli. "It is strong meat. Too strong."

The Kin were used to empty stomachs. Sometimes a Good Place would fail. They would find no game, or there would have been a bush fire that destroyed the plants they'd expected to harvest. Then they would have to travel on, foodless, to the next Good Place. Even the little ones understood that cramming a starved stomach with meat ended with a bellyful of burning stones.

Suth cut away the parts of the fox that people do not eat and told Mana to carry them well away along the slope and leave them there. The rest of the carcass he laid against the foot of the cliff and piled rocks over it to keep it safe. Then he drank again and sat looking out over the burning plain below. Somewhere out there what was left of the Kin was moving farther and farther away. Soon they would be dead, in the burning desert. He would never see them again.

Another thought came to him. No. We six children, on this hillside—we are what is left of the Kin.

He looked at the others. Tinu, so skinny and small, so ashamed of her odd face and speech that she had never dared be anyone's friend. But smart all the same—the trick she had done with the twig in the crack showed that. Little Po, who had always made everyone laugh—almost as soon as he could walk he was trying to swagger like a man. Mana. Suth realized he knew almost nothing about Mana, had barely noticed her before now, she was so quiet, though he had known her since she was born. Otan, lying asleep in Noli's lap. He was still too small to know or guess much about. And Noli herself...

When had Moonhawk begun to visit her in her dreams? Suth wondered. He had never heard of any of the First Ones coming to a child, not in any of the Kins. He knew Noli well. His father and hers had been brothers. He had played with her since they were babies, walked beside her as the Kin journeyed from one Good Place to the next. She'd never said anything about Moonhawk visiting her in her dreams. But then, half a moon ago, she'd woken them all where they lay by springing to her feet in the darkest part of the night and shrieking about the strangers, the cruel fighting, the blood...

And Bal had cursed her, and said she was only a stupid child having a nightmare. When her shrieks had gone on, he'd struck her. He had seen nothing.

But three days later, as they gathered for their evening meal, the strangers had attacked.

Suth thought of a time when he had been small. The Kin had come to a place called Ragala Flat, and had found another Kin, Weaver, already there. There had been great feasting, and giving of gifts. But while the fire had still burned bright, Bal and an old man from the Weaver Kin had gone off together into the dark.

"Where does Bal go with that old man?" Suth had asked his father.

His father had made a sign, putting his palm to his mouth.

"They go to talk dream stuff," he had muttered. "It is a thing that is not spoken of. It is secret."

As he had grown older Suth had realized that in each of the Kins there was one person like Bal. Their own First One came to that person in dreams. It didn't need to be the leader, though Bal was. It could be a man or a woman. But it was never a child. How could it be? And yet Noli…

She was looking at him as if she'd guessed his thoughts, but all she said was, "What must we do now, Suth?"

"We rest," he answered. "All are tired. We have water. We have meat for three days."

"The meat is too strong," she said. "Soon the small ones are sick. They must have plant stuff."

"Yes. All that below is bitter bush, I think. Let us look."

Leaving the little ones in the shade of the cliff, they climbed down the gully, but as they had thought only one sort of shrub seemed to grow there, with twisted gray branches and round, fat leathery leaves. It was common in dry places, but the Kin did not eat it. Experimentally Suth nibbled a leaf, and spat. The harsh taste stayed in his mouth a long while despite a lot of rinsings with water from the crack.

Tired from their night's walk they slept through the middle of the day, but were woken by Otan's crying. He was hungry again, and so were they all, so Suth fetched out the carcass of the fox. Ants had found it, but he brushed them away and butchered more meat, though again he wouldn't let anyone eat more than a few mouthfuls.

"Today we rest," said Suth. "Tomorrow we go."

"Where do we go?" said Noli.

"I do not know. Perhaps Moonhawk sends you a dream," said Suth.

"Perhaps," said Noli.

He was too anxious to sleep. They could

not stay here long. If they tried to follow Bal across the desert they would die. If they tried to go back through Dry Hills they would almost certainly die too. The Kin had only made it as far as they had because they had set out with full water gourds. Suth's little group had none.

Restless, he rose and went to explore along the slope. There might be more water seeping out of the cliff, with good plant stuff feeding from it. That would at least allow them to stay here a few more days, until the little ones became stronger.

It didn't look promising. The slope became steeper, and changed to dangerous scree—a great stretch of loose rocks ending far below in what looked like another cliff. He tossed a rock down. It dislodged another, and between them they started a small avalanche, which went rumbling out of sight. No, not this way, he decided, and went back to the others.

Noli was awake, trying to comfort Po, who had gobbled his meat without chewing it enough and was whining about a stomach ache.

"Did Moonhawk come?" Suth asked.

"No," she said.

He lay down, more anxious than ever, trying to remember any details he could about the journey across Dry Hills. But he had been in his trance of shock then, hardly noticing what happened around him, so all he could recall was endless thirsty trudging across hot stony ground, with rough slopes rising on either side, and no sign of food or water anywhere.

As the sun went down he was still worrying about this, lying on his back and gazing up at the sky, hard blue all day, but now paler, grayer, and turning golden toward the west.

Out of that sky he saw a flock of birds descending, circling around and around, wings spread, coming nearer and nearer until they disappeared behind the rim of the cliff.

Suth's spirits rose. This was something he had seen before. There was a Good Place called Stinkwater, which the Kin had used to visit at two special seasons. At other times it was a useless marsh, its water black and foul. But then at the good seasons the birds came spiraling down out of the sky, countless, tens beyond tens beyond tens, some so weak and tired with long flying that they were easy to catch. Several Kins would gather at those times at Stinkwater, and there would be fine eating for everybody.

Noli too had seen the birds and had thought the same thought.

"There is a Good Place up there," she said.

"We look for a way tomorrow," he said, "when we go back through Dry Hills."

Oldtale

Monkey Makes Fire

Snake and Crocodile and Fat Pig and the others came to Monkey and said, "Why do you eat our food and drink our water and sleep in our caves and disturb us on our crags with your chattering when you have made nothing of your own?"

Monkey said, "Very well. I am cleverer than you are. Now I do something better than any of you."

He thought for a day and a night and a day, and then while Black Antelope slept, he looked at the sky and saw a great cloud that covered the moon.

Then Monkey clapped his hands, and so great was the sound that the cloud burst and fire fell out and poured down to the earth and burned the trees and the grasses and dried up the water holes and smote the crags where Moonhawk perched and shriveled the roots on the ground, and only Little Bat was safe in her caves.

Little Bat looked out and saw what was being done, so she flew to where Black Antelope slept and squeaked in his ear, "Monkey is killing our Good Place with fire. Stop him."

Black Antelope woke and he too saw what was being done. He reared up and breathed through his nostrils and blew out the fire.

He called to Monkey to come, and Monkey was afraid, and hid. But Moonhawk spied him from her crag and told Snake, who went softly and coiled himself around Monkey and caught him and carried him to Black Antelope.

Black Antelope said, "You have done bad things. Now I make your skin itch like fire. You do not eat or drink or sleep until you have put all to rights, as it was before."

Then with his skin itching like fire Monkey set to work, but he could not do it. He poured water into the holes, but it was salty and sour. He put roots into the ground, but they made Fat Pig sick. He grew trees, but they were too thorny for Weaver's wives to nest in, and their fruits fell to the ground before they were ripe.

In the end Monkey came to the others and said, "I cannot do this. You must help me."

They said, "What do you give us in return?"

Monkey said, "I have nothing to give."

They said, "You give this. You are servant and slave for a whole moon to each of us in turn."

So they agreed, and all in their ways made that Place good again, with clean water and fine trees and grasses and sweet nuts and fruits and roots, and in exchange Monkey worked for each of them in turn, doing whatever he was told from morning till night for a whole moon. He did not like this at all.

One day, while he was catching insects

for Little Bat, Monkey smelled smoke. He looked and found a spark of the fire he had made still smoldering. He fetched dry leaves and blew on the spark and fed the leaves into it until he had fire again. Then he found a hollow log and sealed the ends with clay and put the fire in the middle and made the first fire log, which he hid in a secret place.

When all the work was done Monkey went to Black Antelope and said, "Look. Now our Good Place is as it was before."

Black Antelope looked, and saw it was true. But he did not see where Monkey had hidden the fire log. Then he breathed on Monkey and made his skin clean.

Only one small patch under his armpit still itched like fire. That was because of the fire log.

And that is why Monkey is always scratching.

3

They slept well away from the water, in case a fox or some other hunter came to drink in the night. Suth and Noli piled rocks around a nook in the cliff to make a small lair where they could huddle, and nothing disturbed them.

In the morning Suth let them eat more meat and told them to drink as much as their stomachs would hold. While they did he cut off a leg of the fox to carry with them, breaking his cutter as he wrestled with the tendons of the joint. When he had finished he looked for Noli, but couldn't see her. Tinu had gone back to sleep. Mana was playing a pebble game with little Otan. Po was banging two rocks together, trying to make his own cutter.

"Where is Noli?" Suth asked.

Mana pointed along the cliff and he saw her, far beyond shouting range, picking her way across the dangerous rock-covered slope.

He was angry. The morning was already hot. They had far to go, back along the way they had come, before they could begin to look for a way to climb to the top. This was not how a leader should be treated. He would have words to say to Noli.

When at last she came back he rose and went to meet her, without thought hunching his shoulders and shaking his mane out to show her his anger. She answered by kneeling and pattering her hands on the ground in front of his feet.

"I found a way up the cliff," she said.

He heard and understood, but his shoulders and neck stayed rigid and his lips taut across bared teeth, as if he had been Bal. It wasn't anything he was doing on purpose. His body did it to him, because he was angry. Then he relaxed, and laughed, and helped her up.

"Moonhawk showed you?" he said.

"No. But...it is hard....I was...pulled."

He didn't understand. "Perhaps it was Moonhawk," he suggested.

"Perhaps."

"Good. Show me."

He let Noli lead the way, with Otan on her hip, and Po, Mana, and Tinu in single file behind her. He went last to make sure the little ones moved with care. When they reached the slope of loose stuff where Suth had turned back last night, Noli started to pick her way across. Suth made the others wait, and then follow well apart, moving one at a time, testing each foothold.

But it was Suth himself who fell. A rock twisted under him. He felt himself going, as if the whole hillside was sliding away beneath him, and flung himself flat with his arms reaching sideways, then lay there, gasping, while the avalanche he had started roared away beneath him. He rose and saw with relief that the others were all safe and waiting for him, though their eyes were still wide with fright.

They moved on, more carefully than ever, until the cliff seemed to come to an end.

Noli edged her way around the corner and disappeared. Then Mana, then Tinu, then Po. Suth came last of all and saw what Noli had found.

It was as if the mountain had been broken apart, and the two pieces had shifted against each other, leaving a crack between them. The ledge that the children were standing on led into the crack.

"See," said Noli. "It is the same as Tarutu Rock."

Tarutu Rock was a huge isolated crag, which the Kin had used as an overnight lair. It had a dew trap nearby. The rock was a flat-topped pillar, which could only be climbed by a deep crack running up one side. This crack was like that, only far, far higher.

Suth gazed up, hesitating. The small ones might need to be carried some of the way. Suppose they all got stuck....

But he knew in his heart that the journey back through Dry Hills would be just as dangerous. They might all die of thirst on the way. While somewhere up above this cliff there was a good chance of finding water.

Why else should those birds have settled down last night?

And besides, Noli had said she was "pulled" to find this crack....

He clambered into it. The rock surface felt faintly moist. The crack faced away from the sun, and its depths would be in shade until the evening. That decided him.

"We try," he said.

The climb was very slow and tiring. They had Otan to carry. Tinu was still weak from her fever. And though the little ones were used to scrambling up to lairs, they still needed help in the difficult places—though Po, of course, kept wanting to prove that he could manage all on his own. At least they were mostly in shade, and a slight breeze flowed down the crack, cooled by the chill in the rock.

At last, when the sun was so high that the rocks in the desert cast no shadow, Suth looked up and saw only sky above them. This stretch of climbing had been easy enough for the small ones to manage almost without help. Mana was just ahead of Suth, then Noli with Otan, then Po and Tinu.

"Wait, Mana," said Suth. "I go see."

He scrambled past her and put his head cautiously out into the open. To his disappointment he found that they hadn't reached the top after all, only a wide ledge with more cliff rising above it.

He was just clambering out when he heard a harsh cry and a sudden movement to his right. He looked and saw a large bird, some kind of eagle, launching itself away from an untidy heap of twigs on the ledge. For a moment he thought it had flown off, scared by his sudden appearance, but then he heard shrill cheepings from among the twigs and at the same time saw the eagle wheel around and come hurtling in to defend its nestlings. Rapidly he ducked back into the crack.

"Hide! Hide!" he shouted. "Eagle comes!"

Luckily the crack at this point was deep and narrow. As the eagle rushed closer, Suth huddled back gripping the fox leg by its shank and holding it ready to strike. The bird was into its attack attitude, with its great hooked talons stretched in front of it, when at the last instant it realized that it couldn't get at its target without crashing its wings into the cliff on either side.

Somehow it managed to stop itself in mid-flight and turn and soar upwards, but at once it swung back and came plunging down to get at Suth from above. There was no hope of fighting it off, so he cowered down and again the narrowness of the crack defeated it.

It attacked again and again from different angles, but at last gave up trying and simply circled with harsh, angry cries above the ledge.

Suth watched it in despair. It was a big, fierce bird, with a vicious beak and talons. A grown man wouldn't have wanted to face it. But the Moonhawks had to cross the ledge. Once inside the crack above they would be safe again.

Somehow he must get out onto the ledge and keep the eagle at bay while Noli and Tinu got the small ones across. What could he use as a weapon? The fox leg wasn't much good. He needed rocks, but where on this sheer cliff...? Ah, yes, a little further down they'd had to work their way past a large boulder that had fallen and wedged itself in the crack. Then smaller stuff had fallen on top of it and lodged there....

"Tinu," he called. "Below you I saw rocks, good for throwing. Bring them. Bring many."

He explained his plan to Noli while Tinu clambered up and down, bringing two or three rocks at a time. She passed them to Noli, who handed them on to Suth. He took them and slid them out onto the surface of the ledge.

Each time he reached up the eagle swung menacingly in, so close that its wing tip almost brushed the cliff as it passed. When he had the last rock in his hand, Suth passed the fox leg down to Noli, made sure he had a good foothold, and then reached up and merely pretended to push the rock out onto the ledge with the others.

The bird swung in and down as before. As it crossed above him, Suth flung the rock with all his strength, catching it full on its body just below the outstretched wing. It gave a sharp squawk and fell away. Instantly Suth scrambled out onto the ledge, picking up two more rocks as he rose. The bird had recovered at once, and was almost on him, coming along the cliff from his right.

His first rock missed. He slung the second and instantly flung himself flat against the cliff. The bird missed its strike.

He jumped to his feet and saw a feather drifting away, so he knew he'd scored another good hit. He snatched up two more rocks and edged closer to the nest, to draw the eagle from the crack. Now that he had rocks, and a place to stand, he felt confident. Rocks were the Kin's main weapon. Like all the children, Suth had practiced throwing them since he'd been big enough to hold them. He was an excellent shot. He stood poised and ready as the eagle attacked again.

This time it seemed to come more cautiously, which was a mistake as that made it an easier target. His first rock struck home and it wheeled away.

"Ready, Noli!" he called.

The bird circled out, turned and swooped towards him. Would it attack yet again? He watched it, panting.

No, the curve of its flight continued, taking it a safe distance from the ledge.

"Come, Mana!" he shouted as it swung away. "Quick! Hide in the crack! Good. Noli, wait! It comes again…Now! Quick!"

Three times more the bird circled past. Each time it swung away a Moonhawk scrambled out of the crack, across the ledge, and into safety. Suth could hear Noli encouraging Mana to climb on, to make room for the others. When Tinu was across, Suth dashed for the crack. Once inside he waited to catch his breath and let his heart stop pounding, and then climbed on.

As he was working his way past Noli they heard a new wild squawking from below. Craning out they saw that there were now two great birds circling by the ledge, calling to each other.

"The mate comes back to the nest," said Noli.

"Noli, you are right," said Suth, sick with the thought of what might have happened if the other bird had come home while he was out on the ledge, with the small ones trying to cross.

Wearily they clambered on, and before very long came out onto a steep rock-strewn slope. Here they rested, and Suth passed the fox leg around for each of them to chew off what they could. Then they struggled on up. There was nothing else to do.

The slope seemed endless. Wherever they could find shade they rested and looked back. Each time they could see more of the desert stretching away beneath them. Never in their lives had they been so high.

"We are climbing into the sky," said Noli.

The sun was hidden beyond the ridge when they came to another barrier, a jagged line of tall rocks, like the teeth of a monstrous crocodile. Here Suth almost lay down and gave up, but he saw the others looking at him for orders, so without a word he explored along the barrier and edged through a gap between two of the rocks. It twisted on itself, and twisted again, and then they were through.

They paused, and caught their breath. At first, with the setting sun in their eyes, it was hard for them to be sure what they were looking at. But then they saw that ahead of

them lay a vast, secret bowl, an ancient vol-
canic crater hidden among the mountains,
ringed by the ridge on which they stood.
The bottom of the bowl was hidden from
them by the slope, but it seemed to be filled
with a light mist. The sun had almost set
and their shadows were long across the slope
before they reached another edge where
they could look down.

Below them, veiled in grayness, lay a
wide green basin. It was not like anything
they had ever seen, so soft, so green, so
misty. Even here, out on the barren slope,
the air smelled of sap and growth.

There had been nothing like this in their
world. The very best of the Good Places
they knew were hot and dry and filled with
glaring sunlight. Young grass that was fresh
and green at sunrise would be tired and
dusty by noon, and the few trees were tough
and twiggy, with small dusty leaves hardened to withstand such heat. They had
never before seen forest. It took Suth a little while to grasp that the strange green
mass that half-filled the bottom of the bowl
was trees.

Noli, standing beside him, sighed.

"It is a Good Place," she whispered. "It is the First Good Place."

All five of them stood and stared. Even Po was silent in wonder.

Oldtale

How People Were Made

Black Antelope said, "It is time for us to make people. Let each give something from which people can be made."

Snake gave two skins, which he had outgrown.

Crocodile gave teeth she had shed.

The Ant Mother gave earth from her nest.

Moonhawk gave the shell of an egg she had hatched.

Parrot gave the shell from one of his wife's eggs.

Little Bat gave some of her droppings.

Fat Pig gave strong hairs from his hackles.

Monkey bit the ball of his thumb and squeezed out drops of his own blood.

"What does Weaverbird give?" said the others.

"Weaver and his wives build the people, because they know how," said Black Antelope.

"And what do you give?" they asked him.

"I give breath," he said.

"What shape do we make these people?" they asked him.

"Let them be long and thin to slither along the ground," said Snake.

"Let them have thick hides and great teeth, to lie in wait in water," said Crocodile.

"Let them be very many and small and quick," said the Ant Mother.

"Let them be fat," said Fat Pig.

"Let them fly through the air with wings," said Little Bat and Moonhawk and Parrot.

"Let them be like me," said Monkey.

"These people are their own shape," said Black Antelope.

Then Weaver summoned his wives and

together they built two people. They broke up Crocodile's teeth to be the bones of two skeletons, and mixed Monkey's blood with the earth from the Ant Mother's nest to be the flesh of two bodies. These they bound around with the two skins that Snake gave. On top they put Moonhawk's eggshell and Parrot's to be the skulls, and filled them with Little Bat's droppings to be the brains. Lastly they added Fat Pig's hackles to be the hair.

Still these people had no shape, only two round bodies with round heads on top. And they did not move or speak.

Then Black Antelope breathed on them, and filled them with his breath, and they grew arms and legs and ears and noses, and fingers and toes formed on their hands and feet. And they woke and stood up.

The one whose skull was a parrot shell was the man, and his name was An. The one whose skull was the shell of Moonhawk's egg was the woman, and her name was Ammu.

The First Ones stood and watched them, to see what they would do, but were not themselves seen, because they had made themselves invisible.

The man and the woman looked around and saw the First Good Place. They looked at each other, and laughed, and were happy.

"These people are like me. They are not like you others," said Monkey. "My blood did that."

4

For a long while the Moonhawks gazed at the great green valley below them. At last Suth gathered his wits, looked at the sun, and saw that it would soon be dark. Hungry and thirsty though they were, this was not the time to explore.

"Night comes," he said. "We must find a lair."

He began to lead them back up the slope, but before they had gone many paces Noli said, "Wait," ran to one side, put Otan down, and kneeled. She took hold of what looked like two small gray rocks, lying against each other amid a jumble of other rocks. Carefully she twisted them loose. They were held to the ground by a thin tough root, which broke after several turns.

Stoneweed. She nibbled around its base until she was able to pull up a flap of thick rind. She took a suck for herself, and another, which she gave, mouth to mouth, to Otan, then passed the plant to Suth. He sucked a little of the dense, oily juice and gave it to Tinu and the little ones. They took their turns without squabbling.

He felt cheered. It was a good sign. Stoneweed was always a lucky find, anywhere. Its juice was strong, and gave strength, as well as quenching thirst, though if even a grown man drank a whole one he would become dazed and stupid.

They climbed back almost to the ridge, looking for some natural lair, but the ground was too open for that, so they huddled against a boulder. Suth and Noli slept with rocks in their hands, but nothing disturbed them.

In the early dawn they rose and went back down to the place where they had stood last evening, and again gazed down on the strange green bowl. There was a new smell in the air, an odd reek, like smoke, but not any smoke that Suth had smelled before.

"Did Moonhawk send you a dream?" he said.

"No," said Noli.

He was disappointed. The more he gazed at what lay below, the more he was afraid. It wasn't ordinary fear, such as fear of a big wild hunter, or fear of Bal when he was angry. Nor was it like a night fear, fear in a bad dream before the horrors begin but the dreamer knows that they are coming.

There were spots in the old Good Places where he had felt a little like this. Tarutu Rock was one. The Kin walked quietly when they came there, and didn't shout or laugh, because it belonged to Little Bat. They would ask her goodwill before they laired there or drank at her dew trap. This place was something like that, but the feeling was far stronger. He stayed rooted where he was, and Noli did the same.

It was Po, too young to feel such things, who started down the slope. At his movement a basking lizard scuttled off a rock. Farther off a ground rat rose on its hind legs to look, then dived into its burrow.

That broke the trance. If there was such game here, there must also be water.

"Come," said Suth, and led the way, peering to the left and right and sniffing the air for danger.

Between the dry slope and the start of the forest lay a belt of scrub—coarse bushes, sometimes growing impenetrably close together, sometimes more scattered. There was no knowing what might be lurking there, let alone in the dark, strange shadows beneath the trees, so Suth led the way along the edge of the belt, moving warily, looking at everything. Where the ground was soft, he stopped and studied it for tracks. He saw several—the scuttlings of ground rats, the slots made by small deer, and the spread prints with a groove between them, where a lizard had passed, dragging its tail. He saw no large paw prints, but he was sure that where there was so much to hunt there must also be hunters. He picked a way around the edge of the soft patches so that the Kin left no tracks of their own. Even on the hard ground, the earth felt faintly moist beneath his feet, as if there had been a heavy dew, though they had slept dry out in their lair on the hill.

"Wait," called Noli from the rear. "I smell juiceroot."

Suth stopped. Yes, there was that thin, bitter odor. He would have noticed it himself if his mind had not been so set on the scents of danger. Exploring down into the scrub they found a bush almost smothered by a straggling creeper with small dull brown flowers. They traced the vines across the ground to the place where they entered the earth. Stoneweed and juiceroot, growing so close together, Suth thought—this was indeed a Good Place.

The ground was too hard to dig with bare hands. With a lot of difficulty they chewed off branches from another bush and made themselves digging sticks with which, morsel by morsel, they began to chip and move the soil away. It was slow work. Among the Kins the men used heavy stone-cutters to make themselves strong digging sticks, and hardened their points with fire. The ones Suth and Noli had made were blunt and weak.

Bit by bit they dug a hole. At last they came to the top of the tuber from which the vine grew, and saw that it was fat and pale. That was good. Juiceroot was different from stoneweed. It was full of water, with a faint bittersweet taste, very refreshing and far nicer than the dribble they'd found running out of the cliff below. After you'd sucked the juice out you could eat the stringy flesh as plant food. It was poor stuff, but better than nothing.

They forgot about anything else. The sweat streamed from them as they worked steadily on, until every muscle ached and their hands were torn and sore. This was how you got juiceroot out of the ground. It took all day, but it was worth the effort.

The little ones understood that too. They had seen it all before, so they sat and watched in silence. Noli broke small pieces from the top of the tuber for them to suck. Time passed. Suth was quite unprepared when Tinu gave the sharp hiss that meant Danger.

He looked up and saw her and the little ones staring beyond him.

He straightened and turned.

Men.

Four of them, standing in a line, just a few paces off. They had digging sticks in their hands. They looked like the men in the Kin, with scars on their cheeks to mark them as grown men and very dark skins. But one of them had eyes of two different colors, dark brown and paler. Shakily Suth rose and faced them. His throat was dry. His heart pounded.

There was no point in fighting, no hope in running. He had done wrong. Even among Kin it would be wrong. Snake didn't dig or hunt in Weaver's Good Places, not without giving gifts, not without many words of asking. Men had been killed for this, and women taken.

He kneeled and spread his hands, palm forward, and bowed his head and then looked up at them. Their faces were unfriendly. The man with strange eyes stepped forward, raising his stick for a blow. Suth did not know if he would strike. It might be only a threat, a warning, but he flinched, and tried to cover his head with an arm.

Noli, from behind him, spoke. "Moon-hawk sent us."

The man hesitated. "Moonhawk?"

He said the name strangely.

"Moonhawk sent me a dream," said Noli.

Another man strode to her, snatched her up by the arm, and shook her.

"Where are your others?" he said. "Where are your grown men? How many?"

He too spoke strangely.

"Five men left only," Noli gasped. "Strangers came. They killed our fathers. We fled."

"These five—they are here?" snarled the man.

"No," said Noli. "I think they are dead. Bal led us to an empty place—no food, no water. Moonhawk came in my dream and said I must come back to the little ones. These. Bal left them behind. Suth came too."

The man who had been about to strike Suth now grabbed him by his hair and hauled him to his feet. He seized his wrist and twisted his arm up behind his back, almost to the breaking point, but Suth didn't struggle or cry out.

The men spoke together. Then two of them stayed to finish digging out the juice-root, while the other two led the children away. The one who was holding Suth kept a grip on his wrist and pushed him on ahead. He felt numb and stupid and helpless, the way he felt on the journey through Dry Hills. His mouth was sour with the taste of failure.

Oldtale

The Children of Ammu

Ammu grew very fat.

She said to An, "I must have meat. Go and hunt."

While An was hunting, Ammu gave birth.

Six and six and six children she had at that first birth.

First she bore three soft eggs. When they opened, Ammu found a boy and a girl in each.

Next she bore three hard eggs. When they opened, Ammu found a boy and a girl in each.

Last she bore six that came from the womb not in eggs, but as the animals that have hair are born. They came from her two and two and two, a boy and a girl together.

Ammu looked at her six and six and six children, and wept.

"How do I feed all these?" she said. "I have only two breasts, and the breasts of An are small, and have no milk."

Now, Black Antelope was far away, grazing on the plains, when Ammu gave birth. But Monkey watched and listened, for he was always curious about people, and all they did. When he heard what Ammu said, he ran to the other of the First Ones and said, "Ammu gave birth to six and six and six children. She cannot feed them all. She has only two breasts."

The First Ones spoke among themselves. They said, "Let us take two each of Ammu's children and care for them, or they will die."

"But what when Black Antelope returns?" said Little Bat. "Then there are none left for him to care for."

"He is the strongest," said Snake. "He gives his strength to those he cares for.

Then they rule all the rest. That is not good."

So they agreed.

They put Ammu into a sleep, and then they drew lots who should choose first which children they should care for. Monkey was clever with his fingers, and he saw to it that he should choose last.

Snake and Crocodile and the Ant Mother chose children who had hatched from soft eggs, and took them from Ammu while she slept.

Weaver and Parrot and Moonhawk chose children who had hatched from hard eggs, and took them from Ammu while she slept.

Little Bat and Fat Pig took children who had been born as the animals that have hair are born, and took them from Ammu while she slept.

Thus only two children were left.

Then Monkey said, "We cannot leave Ammu with no children. Then she weeps worse than before. Let Ammu raise the two who are due to me. Each of you must give me a gift to make up my loss."

They agreed to that, and it was done.

When An returned from his hunting, Ammu showed him the two fine children who were born to them, and they rejoiced.

Ammu said, "While I slept, a strong dream came to me. In my dream I gave birth to ten children, and eight more. I could not feed so many from my breasts. I wept for this. But great animals heard my weeping and came and took all but these two from me."

An said, "It is only a dream," and they laughed together.

When Black Antelope returned and learned what the others had done, he too laughed.

"Monkey has tricked you," he said. "Soon you find what trouble it is to care for the children of people."

5

Suth was careful not to struggle or resist, and after a while the man who held him relaxed his grip a little. He still couldn't see what was happening to the others. He heard one faint whimper from Otan, but small ones learned very early to stay silent in times of danger.

Their narrow path wound through the bushes. Suth's captor moved warily, like a hunter in strange country, pausing often and peering for dangers.

No one spoke. The bare hills were silent. Insects clicked and whirred in the scrub. And all the time birds whistled and squawked in the huge green mass of forest on their right, strange calls that Suth had never heard before.

And then, close by, high up among the branches, something set up a steady whooping cry. He had heard the same call earlier in the distance, but had hardly noticed it because he had been concentrating on things immediately around him. Now, so near, the wild, eerie call made the hair on the back of his neck prickle. Instinctively he froze, but the man who held him twisted his arm and shoved him on, as if he knew the cry meant no danger.

A few small paths branched off, away from the forest, but they kept to the one they were on until it led out toward the bare hillside. Even before they were clear of the scrub Suth's nostrils told him that they were coming to some kind of camp—an old one too, much used, because the smells were so strong, wood smoke and charred meat and a whole tangle of people odors. It was strange. Sometimes the Kin had stayed a moon and a moon in the same spot, but they would never have let their smells build up in such a way.

They came out onto a steep, rocky slope with a line of low cliffs some way up it.

People were moving around below the cliffs. One of them called. They all stopped what they were doing and gathered together. As soon as the newcomers were in earshot several voices rose, shouting questions. This was not how the Kin would have met hunters returning with captured strangers. They would have stood silent behind their leader while he made the formal greetings and asked the questions.

The man who held Suth didn't answer, but pushed him grimly on, past the ashes of a large fire, almost as far as the cliff. Here Suth saw a dark opening in the rock face, beside which an old woman was sitting in the sun. She looked as if she was asleep.

The man forced Suth to his knees. The other Moonhawks were herded around him. They waited in silence, the girls with bowed heads, but Po staring angrily about as if he was ready to fight all these people. Otan clung silently to Noli.

The babble of questions continued until the old woman seemed to wake, and raised her head. Her hair was sparse and white, her skin yellow and blotched and wrinkled.

Both her eyes were filmed over with a gray mess.

Suth had never seen anyone so old. Among the Kin she would long ago have been taken into the desert and left to die, because she could no longer keep up.

"Tell," she croaked.

"Dith speaks," said the man with strange eyes, and Suth realized he was telling her his name because she was blind.

"I went with Mohr and Kan and Gal to dig juiceroot," the man went on. "It was mine. I found it. When the shoots were small and green I marked it with my mark. We drank at the lake. Then we went. These six children were there. They dug my juiceroot. I went to strike the boy. To punish, not kill. The girl spoke of Moonhawk. I changed my thought. Mohr asked, *Do you have others? Do you have grown men?* The girl said, *They are dead.* We spoke among ourselves. Our thought was, *We take these children to Mosu.*"

The old woman considered the matter, nodding and wheezing. Suth's heart thudded. He was horribly afraid of this old woman, even more than he was of the men.

"Let the girl speak of Moonhawk," she croaked.

Noli passed Otan to Tinu and came forward. In front of the old woman she kneeled and pattered her hands on the ground, as she would have done to appease Bal when he was angry. Still kneeling she explained what had happened since the fight with the strangers. The old woman bowed her head and seemed to have fallen asleep again, but when Noli had finished speaking she raised a withered arm and beckoned to her.

Noli crawled forward. The old woman felt her all over, and then pushed her away.

"The boy," she croaked.

Suth rose and went to her. She felt him over with cold, dry, quivering hands, checking nose, eyes, and ears, counting fingers and toes. Then she did the same to Tinu and found her twisted mouth.

"What is this?" she croaked.

Tinu was too scared to speak, but Noli explained that she had been born like that.

"Were others among you so?" asked the woman.

"Only Tinu was so, in all the Kins," said Noli.

The woman shoved Tinu away and went on to the small ones. The people watched, muttering.

Suth studied them. There were ten and a few more. Some were old, and needed a stick to hobble on. Two of the men had eyes of different colors, like Dith's. A young woman had a withered leg. A girl, who was standing beside a pregnant woman, moved her hand and Suth saw that there were flaps of skin between the fingers, like those on the feet of the birds at Stinkwater.

Otan bawled as the old woman felt him over, but quieted when Noli took him back. The people started to move around, as if the examination of these strangers was done. Dith and Mohr left to finish digging out the juiceroot. The sense of danger ebbed away, but Suth stayed tense. He found the behavior of these people very strange. They weren't like anyone he knew.

The pregnant woman came up to admire Otan.

"That is a big voice," she said as if this were a special compliment. "It is the voice of a lucky hunter."

"He is hungry and thirsty," said Noli. "Where is water?"

"You have not drunk?" said the woman, sounding surprised.

"We drank yesterday, in the morning," said Noli.

The woman nodded and went and spoke briefly with the old woman, then called the girl with the strange hands and sent her running down the slope after Dith and Mohr. She reached them just before they disappeared into the scrub. There was an argument, but after a bit they started back up the slope. When they reached the camp they were clearly angry, but Dith said, "Come. Be quick," and led the way down again. Suth took Otan, to give Noli a rest. The girl with the strange hands came too.

"Where do we go?" Suth asked her.

"To the lake," she said, obviously surprised by his not knowing. "Where else is water? What is your name?"

"I am Suth. These are Noli and Tinu. The

small ones are Po and Mana. The one I carry is Otan, who is Noli's brother. We have no fathers, no mothers. Our Kin was Moonhawk, but it is gone."

"I am Sula," she said. "Paro is my mother. She gives birth today, before sundown. My father is Mohr, that one, and the other is Dith. Mosu made them take you to the lake. They are angry about that."

"Why do grown men come?" said Suth. "Do we steal a lake?"

Again she stared at him, astonished that he didn't know.

"All go together to the lake," she said. "The men guard us."

They were on a well-worn trail that went leftward down the slope. As they entered the bushes Mohr dropped back to the rear of the line, and both men raised their digging sticks to a ready position and walked more warily. The trail was wide, and creatures other than people had left their prints in its dust. This was something that Suth had seen before, near water holes in places rich in game, but never so many, nor on a trail that so reeked of people.

This trail lead directly into the trees, out

of the blazing sunlight and into a dark green tunnel where the air was dense with strange odors, sappy new growth, unknown pollens and fungi, decaying litter. The men walked carefully, peering left and right into the shadows between the huge still trunks. It was a world unlike anything Suth had ever known.

He started violently as a flock of green and yellow birds flew chuckling across the path, and then froze, with the hair on his neck prickling erect, as the same weird whooping that he'd heard before rose from somewhere almost overhead.

All five Moonhawks stopped in their tracks. Mana put her hand in Suth's and huddled to his side. Sula, walking close behind, almost bumped into them.

"What makes this noise?" he whispered.

She looked at him a moment as if she didn't want to answer. Then she muttered, "He is called Big Voice. His true name is not spoken."

Suth understood what she meant. The people in two of the Kins, Snake and Crocodile, never spoke about their First Ones by name. Instead they called them

"The Silent One" and "She Who Waits." Was the creature Sula called Big Voice the First One of these people?

Suth smelled the water before he saw it, though it didn't have the usual clean, hard smell he knew. Instead, it smelled like the water they had found seeping out of the cliff two mornings ago. They came to it very suddenly. At one moment they were surrounded by the brooding trees, and the next moment there it was, a long, narrow lake twisting away farther than he could see toward the distant ridges. It was utterly still, and except in the small clearing where they stood, the trees came right down to the water.

Dith raised his right hand with the fingers spread wide apart in a gesture of formal greeting and muttered quietly for a few moments. Suth knew what this meant. When the Kin came to a place that had power in it, such as Tarutu Rock or Lightning Tree, their leader would make their peace with that power before they passed by, or camped there.

Dith moved aside and gestured to the Moonhawks to drink while he and Mohr stood guard. Noli took longer than the others because she was feeding Otan a sip at a time from her mouth. While they waited for her, Suth gazed at the lake. His sense of awe grew steadily stronger. He had never in his life seen such an expanse of water, nor felt such stillness. Nowhere in the world, not even the Rock of Meeting at Odutu below the Mountain, where he would not go until the time came for him to be made a man, could be like this. Perhaps he would never go to Odutu now. But he had seen this place.

Tinu touched his elbow, breaking his trance. She pointed toward the water's edge. There, on a patch of mud, just beyond where they had drunk, was a large paw print. The mark of each broad toe showed clearly. Suth's father had shown him just such a print on a sandbank at Sometimes River.

Now he knew what the men stood guard against.

Leopard.

Oldtale

Odutu Below the Mountain

The First Ones made nests and lairs for the children of An and Ammu, according to their kinds. Thus Moonhawk made a nest of twigs among the crags and carried there the two that she was to care for, and the Ant Mother dug a chamber in the earth for the two that she was to care for. So with the others, according to their kinds.

Only Monkey did nothing. An and Ammu did all that, and he watched.

The First Ones fed the children

according to their kinds. Thus Little Bat fed them upon insects, and Crocodile fed them upon creatures that she caught as she lay in wait. So with the others, according to their kinds.

Only Monkey did nothing. An and Ammu did all that, and he watched.

When the children were grown to the height of a garri bush, the First Ones brought them to Odutu below the Mountain. It was there that An and Ammu had their camp at that season.

The First Ones set the children down a little way from Odutu and told them, "Go to that rock that you see, and find what you find."

The children went forward hand in hand, two and two, while the First Ones watched invisible around. They gave back to Ammu the memory that they had taken from her, and she looked up and saw her children, pair and pair and pair, coming to her out of the bush.

Then she rejoiced that they were given back to her.

And An rejoiced with her, and said,

"This is Odutu below the Mountain. This is our Rock of Meeting. From this day it is sacred. From this day an oath sworn here is an oath forever, and a peace made here is a peace forever."

And it was so.

6

While the Moonhawks were at the lake, Paro had put what was left of the fox leg to roast among the hot embers of the fire. When they returned she gave them other food, soft lumps of yellow stuff and dark strips of sun-dried root, which they chewed until all the nutty flavor was gone, and then spat the rest out. The root was strange to them, but the Kin used to make the same kind of yellow stuff from pounded seed, mixed with water. They ate it eagerly.

When the meat was cooked, Paro hacked the flesh off it with a good strong cutter, and handed it around. It was delicious after days of raw flesh, but their stomachs were tired of meat and they didn't eat much.

When they had finished, Suth signaled to

the others and they all rose and stood in a line in front of Paro, clenched their fists, and knocked their knuckles together three times.

Food was seldom plentiful, so even when it was, one Kin never accepted a meal from a different Kin without the regular ritual of thanks. Sula laughed aloud, as if they'd done something extraordinary. Paro simply smiled, and spread her hands in a vague gesture.

"We have plenty," she said.

This made Suth puzzled and uneasy. The Moonhawks had done what they knew was the right thing, but Sula had answered rudely, and Paro as if they'd done something stupid. Sula had been friendly, and Paro kind, but how could he trust these people if they behaved like that?

"We cannot take and take from your store," he said. "Show me where we can forage for food, and not make others angry."

"It is far," said Paro. "Your small ones are tired, and the baby is heavy to carry."

"They stay," said Suth. "I go with Tinu. But we have no gourd, to carry food home."

"What is gourd?" she asked. "We take leaves, to carry."

She showed him one. It was thick and leathery, and far larger than any he had ever seen. Carefully she turned the ends up and folded it down the middle rib, tucking the folded ends in, and then slid it under her arm. She put the fingers of her other hand together and mimed picking a seed head and dropping it between the two halves of the leaf. Then she handed it to him.

"I cannot come," she said. "My child is almost born. Sula shows you, but she must come back for the birth."

Suth looked at Noli, and she nodded. He felt relieved. This at least was something that was the same among the Kin. If a woman had a daughter and was pregnant again, the daughter must be there at the birthing to see how all was done, so that she would know when her own time came. A mother who bore no more children might ask permission for her daughter to watch when other mothers gave birth. This was important woman lore.

Suth thanked her again, and the three of

them set out, with Sula carrying the bone from the fox leg. Before long they came to a narrow deep ravine. The place reeked. Three vultures rose as they reached the edge. Sula tossed the bone in.

Suth peered over the edge. On the floor of the ravine lay an immense pile of bones, picked clean by scavengers. He was amazed, stupefied. The Kin, of course, used to carry such stuff well clear of wherever they rested, so there was often a scattering of bones ringing their regular camps, but never like this. These people, how long had they lived here to make such a pile? Tens and tens and more tens of rains. They had this one Good Place with so much in it to hunt and forage that they never needed to journey to another. His mind wouldn't think about it. It was too strange.

Sula led them above the line of scrub, until they reached a ground rat warren. Several traps had been set, the kind that Suth had watched his father make—a large rock propped on a triangle of sticks, and baited so that when the bait was moved the sticks gave way and the rock fell. Tinu at once crouched by one of the traps and studied it intently.

"Look," said Sula. "Baga catches a rat. She makes good traps."

"How can you know it is Baga?" said Suth.

"There is her mark," said Sula, pointing to a little pattern of pebbles beside the trap, three in a line and one below. "All her family use this mark. This is Jun's mark. He catches nothing. Do you make a trap? What mark do you choose?"

"Tell me," said Suth.

"Good. You have four like so, and one to the side. You may set your trap here, or in any warren where you see traps. The rats are stupid. They do not learn soon, but when many are caught, the others know not to take the bait. Then we leave that warren and go to another.

"Now I must go back," she added. "I must be with my mother at the birthing. I show you where the others forage."

She led them farther up the hill and turned. From here Suth could see that the forest didn't in fact fill the whole of the bottom of the bowl between the circling ridges. It lay in two wide belts on either side of the lake, which was now visible for most of its length. It stretched a whole day's journey into the distance, an immense, deep crack in the mountaintop, filled with water.

To the left, though, the ground rose and became grassland with patches of open scrub and scattered, flat-topped trees.

"They are there," said Sula.

He looked along her pointing arm and in the far distance saw a line of dark dots. He recognized them at once. No other creatures move or hold themselves in the same way as people.

"My thanks," said Suth.

He didn't have any bait for a trap, so he and Tinu set out, while Sula returned to the camp. As soon as they were picking their way between the areas of scrub, he saw signs of recent foraging. These people were not at all as thorough as the Kin would have been. This was rich country, as good as any of the old Good Places, but there were clumps of grass not stripped of their seed heads, termite nests not dug out, dead branches not stripped for the grubs beneath the bark. But he and Tinu didn't stop for any of the possible pickings. It was important only to do what the others did, and forage where they foraged.

They found the people not working, but resting in the shade of a group of trees. Someone had already come from the cave with news of the Moonhawks' arrival, so they weren't challenged. Several children did rush out to meet them, and then instead of greeting them, stood silent and staring and followed them back to the trees.

A few men were on one side, sitting in a circle and playing some kind of game, and a larger group of women were talking quietly among themselves while they husked seed or fed babies.

The men glanced up and went back to their game. Suth waited, watching them as they in turn tossed pebbles onto a pattern of lines they had drawn in the dust. He assumed that after a while whoever was leader would look up and nod or beckon to him. Then he would kneel and patter his hands on the ground in sign of submission, and ask to be allowed to forage in this people's Place.

Nothing happened. The men continued their game. Tinu, at Suth's side, stood with her head bowed and her eyes down, as if thinking that if she couldn't see anyone then she herself couldn't be seen.

Suth looked around, and a young woman who was sitting against a tree, feeding her baby, smiled at him.

"Who is leader?" he asked her.

She shrugged and frowned, puzzled.

"Mosu?" she suggested.

"Who then do I ask, *May I forage in this Place?*"

"Mosu spoke to Pagi," she said. "Pagi came to us. You may forage with us."

"I thank."

He squatted beside her and Tinu crouched by him, shielding herself from the others with his body. He looked around the group. Not counting children there were ten and ten and ten of them, and a few more. This was a big Kin. Moonhawk at its most had been only ten and ten and a few more. The Crocodile Kin, when they had last met at Stinkwater had been only ten and four. But then, there had been six other Kins beside those two. There were more of these people back at the cave, of course, as well as men out hunting, but still it was not very many if these were the only Kin who ever came here.

Where did they go to find mates? he wondered. The young men of the Moonhawks went to Little Bat and Crocodile to beg a mate, and young men came from Weaver and Parrot to beg from Moonhawk.

"I am Suth," he said. "This one is Tinu. We are Moonhawk."

"I am Loga," she said. "My son is not yet named."

"And what is your Kin?" he asked.

She stared at him, and put her knuckles to her mouth. He realized that he must have said a Thing-that-is-not-spoken, though among the Kin he knew the sign would have been given with the palm of the hand.

"My shame," he muttered, spreading his hands, palm down, in front of his chest, and then slowly lowering them as a sign of pushing the evil back into the earth.

She nodded, but turned away and con-
centrated on her baby.

When they had finished their game, the
men picked up their digging sticks and loped
off along the edge of the scrub. The women
and children moved out into the open,
formed a line and started to forage steadily
across the ground. Almost all of them had
folded leaves under their arms, to carry what
they had gathered. None had a gourd.
Perhaps there were no gourds in the valley.

Suth and Tinu joined the end of the line
and worked steadily. Before the sun was
halfway down the sky they had gathered
enough for their own needs for a full day, but
they had Noli and the small ones to feed
too, so they didn't stop. Suth was crouching
by a clump of spike-grass, stripping off the
ripe seed heads, when he felt a curious sen-
sation, as if the solid ground was trembling
beneath the soles of his feet. It lasted only a
short while and as it ended the whooping
call of Big Voice rose from the forest. Far off,
another answered. The weird cries floated
out over the treetops and away toward the
barren ridges.

The line of foragers stopped work and stood to listen to the call. As it died away, the woman working next to Suth turned and smiled.

"He sings," she said. "Paro gives birth, perhaps. The baby is good. Big Voice is happy for the baby."

The other women seemed to have had the same idea. Without waiting for the men, they started back for the cave.

Po came running to meet them across the last slope. He held up his arms. Suth passed his carrying leaf to Tinu and picked him up.

"You come back," said Po happily.

"I come back," said Suth.

"You father," said Po.

Suth must have looked startled, because Po said it again.

"You father," he insisted. "Noli mother. Mana say this. Yes?"

"Yes," said Suth, slowly. "I am the father now, and Noli is the mother. You are the children, Tinu, Po, Mana, and Otan."

He was still surprised, but in a different way. All along he had been doing his best for the little ones, trying to keep them alive, and find them food and water and safety. But these weren't the only things they needed. They needed a father and a mother too, so they'd chosen Suth and Noli, since there was no one else. And it was Mana who had seen the need.

He thought about her as he carried Po back to the camp. As usual with Mana, Suth hadn't especially noticed it at the time, but now he realized how easy she had made things, as far as she could, ever since he and Noli had rescued the four of them. She hadn't asked for anything, or complained of hunger or thirst or weariness, but she'd watched all the time, and been ready, and kept out of the way when she wasn't needed.

So when he got back to the camp and found Noli sitting with Otan asleep in her lap, and Mana sitting patiently beside her, he put Po down and picked Mana up.

"See, I come back," he said.

She put her arms around his neck and hugged him. Noli looked up and smiled.

"You hear the thing Mana says?" she asked him.

"Yes. It is true," he said.

That evening, when the sun was low, the fire was piled with wood and those who had caught ground rats skinned the bodies for roasting. Then they all trooped down to the lake for their evening drink. Even Mosu came, hobbling on her stick and helped along by the woman with the withered leg, whose name was Foia. This time it was Mosu who raised her hand and spoke in greeting to the water before anyone drank.

On their return they settled in a wide circle around the fire, with the men on one side and the women and children on the other. While they ate, Mohr, who was Paro's mate and Sula's father, carried the new baby around and showed him to everyone in turn. Men as well as women held him and looked him carefully over while he thrashed and squalled, and then passed him back to Mohr.

Mohr didn't show him to the Moonhawks, but Sula brought him proudly over.

"See," she said. "He is whole and clean."

She opened one of the tiny clutching hands and showed that there were four good fingers and a thumb, without webs, like hers, between them. After his mistake with Loga under the shade trees, Suth didn't dare ask what was so wonderful about a child being born normal. Apart from Tinu, all the babies he had known had been born whole and healthy, though later some had fallen sick and died. As it happened, Sula told him anyway.

"When my brother was born he had no arms and no legs," she said. "He would not live. My father carried him into the trees and left him. Our blood is sick. Mosu says, *We are too few. That makes the sickness. We have only each other to mate with*. Now the sickness grows stronger. See. It is here, in me."

She spread her webbed fingers to show him.

"Soon I am a woman," she said. "Then I have you for my mate, Suth. Your blood is good. It gives me good babies. Mosu says this."

Suth smiled uneasily, but she wasn't joking or teasing, though there was always a lot of that among the Kin when children were reaching the right age. He glanced at Noli for reassurance, but she was sitting hunched into herself, breathing heavily, not noticing anything. Tinu was amusing Otan by tickling his feet with a grass stem. Mana was asleep, and Po was playing tag around the circle with a boy his own age. Suth didn't really understand what Sula had told him, but he didn't feel easy about it. Perhaps this was not a Good Place after all. Perhaps it was like the fruit of the sixberry bush, which tasted so good in the mouth that you wanted to eat more and more, but when you'd had more than five it caused you to vomit until you thought you would die.

Sula carried the baby away and gave him to Paro. Po returned panting and bright eyed from his game. Noli gave a shuddering sigh and sat up and looked around.

"You hear the thing that Sula says?" Suth asked her.

She shook her head and in a low voice he told her. She nodded.

"I slept and did not sleep," she said. "Moonhawk came. She told what Kin these are. They are Monkey. Big Voice is Monkey."

He stared at her, remembering what the Oldtales said.

"Monkey has no Kin," he said.

"These are Monkey," she insisted. "Does Moonhawk lie?"

Oldtale

How Sorrow Came

An and Ammu journeyed through all of the First Good Places with their children. They showed them the trails and the water holes and the dew traps and the warrens. They told them the names of the plants, root and fruit and nut and leaf, those that were good to eat and those that were bad. They showed them the places of safety and the places of danger.

They came to a tree that held the nests of weavers, and An cut a long pole and showed how to knock down the nests, so as to eat the eggs and the young chicks.

Then the two who had been reared by Weaver said, "We may not eat of this food. We are of the Kin of Weaver." Their names were So and Sana.

They came to a warren below the crags where moonhawks nested, and Ammu showed how to set traps for ground rats.

Then the two who had been reared by Moonhawk said, "We must set the hearts aside for Moonhawk. This is her prey, and we are of the Kin of Moonhawk." Their names were Nal and Anla.

They came to a cave and An said, "Here we sleep."

Then the two who had been reared by Little Bat said, "First we must ask leave of the bats who lair in the cave. We are of the Kin of Little Bat." Their names were Tur and Turka.

And so with each of the others in their turn, each honoring the First One who had raised them.

Only the two who had been reared by An and Ammu themselves had no knowledge of any Kin to which they belonged, because Monkey had hidden himself and done nothing for them. Their names were Da and Datta.

They came to An and said, "Our brothers and sisters have each a Kin, but we have none. How is this?"

An, knowing no better, said, "You were reared by Ammu and by me. You are of the Kin of People."

It was from this that all sorrow came.

7

They slept in the cave. It stank. Like the Kin these people didn't make dung or pass water close by their lairs, but went well away to do so. But small children can't control their bowels all night, and though the people piled up grass and brought it in for bedding and cleared it out when it was dirty, the reeks gradually gathered in the cave until in the nostrils of the Moonhawks the stench seemed almost too strong to bear. The people didn't seem to notice or mind, any more than they noticed the strange foul-egg odor that wafted to and fro in the valley.

The stink in the cave was made worse because when all were in for the night, the people piled rocks across the entrance, blocking it to the height of a man's shoulder. That meant any who needed to go out to relieve themselves were unable to do so.

Suth wondered if this was necessary, but on that very first night he got his answer. In his sleep he sensed a stirring, and woke and heard a low snarl, followed by another, coming from outside the cave. Night hunters were there, squabbling over scraps of food left from the meal. Against the patch of sky above the barrier, Suth saw the outlines of men with digging sticks raised ready to fight an intruder. Nothing more happened. The animals moved away and everyone relaxed back into sleep.

Later he woke again. He had felt the rock beneath him shudder, twice, but no one else in the cave stirred. They must be used to that.

The barrier was taken down as dawn was breaking, and the rocks laid aside to be used again. The air smelled wonderfully fresh and clean after the cave. They ate a little food and then went down to the lake for their morning drink. After that the foragers and hunters left, but Noli was still feeding Otan so the Moonhawks stayed for her.

While they waited the air grew heavy. Clouds gathered, seemingly from nowhere. Everyone left at the camp hurried into the cave. There was a clap of thunder, and rain came pelting down while the lightning blinked and the thunder rumbled on and on. And then it was over, and the whole hillside was streaming with water.

This was the season of thunderstorms. The Kin used to watch them grumbling across the plains, dropping their rain in one place and not in another. But Suth had never seen one like this, gathering and gone so soon, and all in one place. It was very strange.

As the Moonhawks were getting ready to leave, Foia, the woman who helped blind old Mosu move around, came up.

"You speak now with Mosu," she said.

Suth frowned. The old woman made him very uneasy, and he wanted as little to do with her as he could. He glanced at Noli.

"I come also," she said, and passed Otan to Tinu to mind.

Mosu was in her usual place by the cave, with her back against the cliff. Suth and Noli kneeled before her and pattered their hands on the ground.

"The boy comes," said Foia. "The girl also."

She moved a short distance away and sat down.

Mosu gave no sign of having heard, but then she raised her head and said in her croaking voice, "You are children. You have no father and no mother."

"The strangers killed our fathers," said Suth. "They took our mothers."

"No mother, no father—the child dies," said Mosu. "Now I give each of you a mother and a father. They care for you and teach you our ways."

For a moment Suth didn't understand what she meant. Then he realized that she wanted to split the Moonhawks up and give them each to a different family.

He looked anxiously at Noli. She drew her lower lip into her mouth and let it go. *This is not good*, she was telling him. He remembered what Mana and Po had been saying last evening, that he was now their father, and Noli their mother.

I will not let this happen, he thought. *But I must not offend this old woman. She is the leader in this place.*

"We thank," he said hesitatingly. "But... we are not of this Kin. We are Moonhawk. Our ways are ways of Moonhawk."

"Moonhawk is dead," said Mosu. "All those Kins are dead, gone. All your Good Places are taken. There is no Snake, no Fat Pig, no Ant Mother. There is only one Kin, and it is ours. Big Voice sings in the forest. He says this to me."

"He is a liar!" said Suth, suddenly too angry to be careful. He felt his scalp move as his hair bushed out in his anger.

"He is a liar, I say!" he repeated. "Everyone knows this. Moonhawk came to Noli. Last night she came, while we ate. She told whose Kin you are. She is not dead."

Mosu merely cackled.

"Do your small ones live many more moons?" she said. "Does your baby live, that cannot walk? Can the girl feed the baby. Has she milk in her breasts?"

She rocked to and fro, wheezing between her cackles.

Suth looked at Noli for help, but she didn't see him. Something was happening to her. Her eyes were wide and blank, and her whole body shuddered.

"Monkey is sick," she said in a deep, gasping voice. "Moonhawk speaks this. Monkey is sick."

She staggered as if she'd been struck, and Suth caught her to stop her falling. He held her while she shuddered once more and gave a slow, exhausted sigh. Then she drew herself clear and stood normally.

At first Mosu didn't seem to have heard what she'd said, but her cackling died away and she sat still, wheezing heavily. Suth remembered what Sula had told him last night.

"Your blood is bad," he said. "Your men have eyes of two colors. Your children have skin between their fingers. Your babies have no arms, no legs. You want our good blood. I, Suth, say this. Moonhawk lives. We are Moonhawk. You take us one from the others. You make Moonhawk die. I say you can not do it. I say we leave this place and go far and far. You can not have our good blood."

Mosu muttered something and seemed to shrink into herself.

They waited. At length she raised her head and sighed.

"Big Voice is not a liar," she said quietly. "He is a trickster. His words say this and that. Long, long, he sings to me. Before my sons are born he sings to me. Their sons are soon men. I know the ways of Big Voice. He says this and that."

"Moonhawk is Moonhawk," said Suth. "Our Kin lives. We stay one Kin, together."

Mosu cackled briefly.

"Are you a man?" she said. "Can you care for four children? Do you make a digging stick? Do you harden it in the fire? Do you fight the leopard when it comes for your small ones? Do you sit with the men at the feast? Do you speak when they speak?"

"In three moons I am made a man," said Suth obstinately.

This was true and not true. If the strangers hadn't come and changed everything, then in three moons the Kin would have traveled south to Odutu below the Mountain, and Suth would have spent a night alone on the Mountain above Odutu, and in the morning Bal would have cut the first man-scar into his cheek and told him to make himself a digging stick. After that he would have left the women's side and sat with the men and listened to their talk. But it would have been tens of moons and three more scars before he would have been allowed to join in.

"Always the men mock this boy-man. They point fingers. They raise their lip," said Mosu.

"Stones are sharper," he answered.

She turned her head away.

"Make a digging stick," she said.

"Moonhawk is Moonhawk," he insisted.

"You say it," she answered. "Go forage. The girl stays. We talk."

He looked at Noli.

"I talk with Mosu," she said. "Bring Otan to me."

As Suth left the camp with Tinu and the small ones, he saw Noli sitting cross-legged, with Otan in her lap, listening while Mosu talked. He felt puzzled and angry. He had just stood up to the old woman and won his point. Moonhawk wasn't going to be split up. They were keeping together. Only they weren't, because Noli wasn't coming to the foraging grounds with them, but was staying behind to talk to Mosu.

She had to stay. Suth understood that. Mosu was leader of these people. If Noli had tried to refuse, Mosu would have kept her there by force. But Suth guessed Noli actually wanted to stay, he didn't know why. That was what hurt.

On the way to the ground rat warren, Suth broke branches from bushes to use in his trap. He had noticed a pile of good flat rocks by the warren, which people must have carried there to use, but they didn't seem to be marked with anyone's mark so he took one of those. Po, of course, wanted to build a trap too, so Suth broke a spare branch into lengths for him, as a father would have done. He showed him how to use them to prop the rock up, so that when a ground rat nibbled the bait a stick would be dislodged, and the rock would fall and kill the rat. It wasn't easy, and Suth didn't think either of them would have much luck.

Meanwhile Tinu and Mana built a trap of their own. All three were baited with seed paste mixed with the crushed leaves of a garri bush, which ground rats were especially fond of. When they'd finished, they marked the traps with the Moonhawk mark· and set off for the foraging grounds.

The foragers weren't where they'd been yesterday, but Suth found them easily enough by the noise they were making, down in the thicker scrub. They were hunting for a kind of caterpillar that came out of the ground on the morning after a rain and climbed a bush and hung itself from a thread, to begin the process of turning itself into a moth. Only on the first morning was it good to eat, Sula told Suth. By evening the case it spun around itself had begun to harden, and the flesh inside was too bitter to swallow.

While the foragers searched they kept up a constant yodeling, passing it to and fro along the line. The men didn't join in. They just stood guard, striding around at the edge of the group, letting out hoarse shouts and thwacking at the bushes with their digging sticks. Every now and then one of the foragers would bring one of them a caterpillar, pinch off its head and pop the body into the guard's mouth.

Po was delighted by the shouting and thwacking and ran around yelling at the top of his voice until one of the women caught him and brought him back to Suth.

"You keep him close," she said scoldingly. "You want a leopard to take him?"

"I thank," said Suth meekly. He realized that however bravely he had spoken to Mosu, he had a lot to learn about being a man and caring for his family in this new place.

The caterpillars were delicious and plentiful, and they ate all they could, pinching the heads off, because that was where the bitterness came from. When the taste began to change they gave up and moved into the open, but before they had formed their foraging line, a man came running from the distance. While he was still some way off he stopped and made signs, and without a word spoken all the men in the party ran off to join him. Suth watched them lope silently out of sight in single file.

"What happens?" he asked Sula.

"Men hunt deer," she said. "We make no noise."

He understood at once. The men of the Kin also hunted deer when they got the chance, but they didn't often kill one, except at a Place called Mambaga, where at the right season deer passed through in great numbers, and several Kins joined to hunt them as they crowded together to cross a particular dry gully. Usually it was a matter of the best hunters lying in wait, and the others trying to drive the deer to that point. But deer were quick and tricky. Mostly they ran somewhere else.

Now the foragers moved into shade and sat quietly until the hunters came back dejectedly. The hunt, it seemed, hadn't really begun. The deer had run off before the ambush was properly set. So the men settled down to their game, while the foragers went back to work. Once again Suth was struck by how much there was to gather, and what a rich, easy living these people had here.

Perhaps it was because Monkey had made this Place for them, he thought. Monkey was clever. Everyone knew that.

On their way back to the camp that evening, they stopped at the warren to pick up their catch. But, although several traps had been sprung, only the one that Tinu and Mana had made had caught a rat.

The women, of course, seized the chance to jeer at the men. These mighty hunters couldn't catch deer. They couldn't even catch ground rats. A couple of girls could catch a ground rat, but the men couldn't.

The men didn't like it. They were still sore about missing the deer. Dith looked at the trap with the Moonhawk mark beside it, and then his eye was caught by Suth's and Po's, not far off, and marked the same.

He turned angrily on Suth.

"No girl made this trap," he said. "The boy made it. See, he made three. You! Boy! You set three traps. This is bad. Each must set one trap only."

He glared at Suth with his shoulders hunched and his hair bushed, but Suth was angry too. He couldn't stand up to a grown man, but he refused to go into the full submission ritual of kneeling and pattering his hands on the ground. He just bowed his head and fluttered his fingers for a moment in the air.

"I built this one," he said. "Po built that. See, it is a child's, a small one's. Mana. Speak true. Who made this trap?" There was no point in asking Tinu herself. They wouldn't have understood what she was trying to say. And in any case she would have been utterly tongue-tied.

"Tinu made this trap," said Mana sturdily. "She knew the way. I watched."

The women jeered again, and picked Tinu up and held her high in triumph. She hated it and tried to cower into herself until they put her down. When the fuss had died away, Suth took her aside and praised her quietly, but she hid her face even from him.

That evening as they sat around the fire, Suth asked Noli about her talk with Mosu. He was hoping she might have learned something useful about these people and their ways.

She was feeding Otan and didn't answer right away, but then she looked up with her face smeared with the mixture of seed paste and berry juice she had been chewing for him. She shook her head.

"Do not question me, Suth," she said. "I, Noli, ask this. It is secret."

Suth was hurt. He knew that people to whom the First Ones came sometimes talked among themselves about how it was, and not to anyone else. Yes, Noli was one of those people, but that wasn't all Noli was.

He turned his head away and stared at the fire. He needed Noli. Didn't she understand? He was a boy, but he must pretend to be a man and stand up to the men as he had stood up to Dith at the warren. How else could he care for his family? *Their* family. If he was the father, she was the mother. Would she spend all her time talking secrets with the old woman? This was not right.

He felt her fingers touch his arm, and her hand move down to rest on the back of his hand and hold it. Still he would not look at her.

"I tell you this, Suth," she said in a low

voice. "These people keep us here. They are sick. Their blood is bad. Soon we are men and women. Then they choose us for mates. They have our good blood. They are sick no more. All this Mosu tells them. But they think. If we are together, all six, perhaps we go secretly away. Can they watch all the time? That is difficult. Can they keep us in the cave? Then we fall sick, we die. So Mosu says, *Let Noli stay with me. Suth does not go without Noli.*"

Now Suth stared at her, appalled. Without thought he began to rise to his feet, as if he meant to gather the Moonhawks and lead them away, then and there, away from these people, out of this trap. Noli tightened her grip on his hand and pulled him down.

"They watch," she muttered. "Be clever, Suth. Be secret."

Oldtale
Da and Datta

The sons of An and Ammu strove among themselves to see who was best. They wrestled, and raced, and threw rocks at a mark, and such things.

And one was strongest, and one was swiftest, and one was keenest of sight, each according to the nature of the First One who had reared him. But Da was none of these things.

"I am still the best of you," said Da.

The others mocked him and said, "How are you the best of us, when those who cared for us made us stronger and swifter and keener of sight than you?"

Da said, "I was cared for by People, and they made me best. People are above creatures."

They said, "How so?"

To this Da had no answer, and they mocked him again, until he ran weeping into the desert.

There he found Datta, and told her what had been done and said, and she wept also.

They slept, and Monkey came to Datta in a dream.

In the morning she said to Da, "Go to your brothers and say thus and thus."

Da went to his brothers and said, "Now I tell you how I am the best of you. I eat of the flesh of all creatures, as I choose, and their eggs also. But for each of you there is one creature whose flesh you do not eat, nor its eggs.

"Weaver cared for So. Does So eat the eggs of weavers? Ant Mother cared for Buth. Does Buth dig the nests of ants for their grubs? Fat Pig cared for Gor. Does Gor track the sow to her lair and eat of the tender piglets? And so with the rest of you. I do all of these things.

"But who eats of the flesh of those who took care of me? None of you does this. None of you eats of the flesh of People. People are best. I, Da, say this.

"Lowest are rocks and earth and water. Next above them are plants. Next above plants are creatures. Next above creatures are People. They are highest."

They had no answer to this, but they mocked him all the same and threw dirt at him and drove him away, and he wept.

Monkey was angry when he saw what was done to Da. He came to Datta in a dream, and showed her where he had hidden the fire log that he had made.

Da and Datta went to that place and found the fire log. They made fire and roasted the flesh of lizards and ate it, and it was very good.

They roasted more and took it to their brothers and sisters and gave it to them. Then the others lusted for roast flesh and said, "Give us the fire log. Then we too can make fire and roast what we catch."

Da and Datta said, "First you must come to the Rock of Meeting at Odutu below the Mountain and swear that we are best, because we were cared for by People. And you must swear that henceforth our ways shall be your ways, because they are the ways of People."

Such was their lust for roast flesh that the others agreed. They came to Odutu below the Mountain and swore upon the Rock of Meeting as Da and Datta had told them. Then Da and Datta gave them fire, and they made fire logs, one for each Kin.

But when An and Ammu learned what had been said and done, they wept.

8

A moon went by, and another, with a thunderstorm every few days. The storm season ended and more moons went by.

Otan could walk. The valley was no longer strange to him. It was as if he had always lived here, being taken down to the pool morning and evening to drink, and at night sleeping in the stinking cave.

It was the same with Mana and Po. They quickly learned the ways of these people, and made friends with their children and joined in their games. Po was a favorite with the women, who spoiled him and told him what a fine boy he was. No one paid much attention to Mana.

They paid even less to Tinu. They seemed to think that because she couldn't talk clearly she wasn't a real person. She didn't seem to mind. She spent some of her time helping Noli with Otan, but most of it tagging along with Suth, watching what he did and helping him when she could. She set a trap at the warren almost every time they passed it, and usually caught something. She built better traps even than Baga, with delicately balanced rocks that dropped at a touch.

The men, of course, wouldn't admit this. They said it was because she was Moonhawk, who preyed upon ground rats. That was why Tinu was lucky.

(These people told many of the same Oldtales as the Kin, but some were different. There were nine Kins, of course, because Monkey had one. In the Oldtales they called Monkey by his real name. It wasn't Monkey, they said, who'd caused all the trouble. It was Crocodile and Fat Pig, who were jealous of his cleverness because they were stupid. They'd conspired against him.)

Unlike Tinu, Noli seemed to have changed. She remembered the Good Places, of course, and the long journeys between them, but she didn't mind their loss. After the first few days Mosu allowed her to come foraging sometimes with the rest of them, but once they were back at the cave Noli would spend much of the time sitting with Mosu, listening or talking, or else in what seemed to be a kind of shared half trance, as if they were dreaming the same dream.

"What do you do with that old woman so long?" Suth asked her.

"I learn," she said. "She is very old. She knows much."

Suth didn't like this. He missed Noli. He needed her. She was Moonhawk, not Monkey. She belonged with him, raising their small ones in the true Moonhawk ways. Mosu had power. She must have, to be leader of these people. Ant Mother sometimes had women for leaders, and so did Snake, in the Oldtales, but never since anyone could remember, and never old and blind, like Mosu. Was she using her power to trap Noli, to make her become not Moonhawk but Monkey?

"She sees nothing," he said crossly. "Her eyes are dead."

"It is because she is old," said Noli. "It is

not the blood sickness. When she was young she saw well. She says long ago tens and tens and tens of people lived in this place. Some lived here, at this cave. Some lived over there. That is where Mosu was born."

She pointed out across the forest to the wide, promising slopes on the far side of the valley. Nobody foraged or hunted there. It was too far to go and return in a day, when there was enough within reach to give them all a good living here. And how would they be safe outside the cave with the big night prowlers around?

The mere sight of those empty spaces made Suth restless. Like the others he had grown used to the valley, but only in certain ways. Almost every day he felt the earth tremble, but now he no longer paused in what he was doing. If it happened at night, it didn't wake him. And he barely noticed the wafts of foul-egg odor that drifted to and fro on the breeze.

On the other hand, the cave still stank in his nostrils. Every evening he entered it with reluctance, wishing there were other places to lair, and in his dreams he walked and walked and walked, and would wake with his legs aching from the imaginary journey. All the life he had known had been moving from one Good Place to the next, following the rains as they moved across the parched land. He could not get used to staying in this one place, going out in the same direction every day, never more than half a morning's journey, to forage the next patch of ground and smell the same smells and see the same horizons as yesterday.

And time and time again something happened to remind him that Noli had been right: he and the Moonhawks were prisoners in this valley. Nobody seemed to bother much about them while they were separated from each other, but as soon as they were all together they were watched. They weren't allowed to forage at the end of the line, where they might drift away unnoticed, but were made to stay in the middle. And if by any chance they got out of sight, somebody came to look for them.

Suth tested this the first time he had a chance. They had hardly started to forage one morning when a storm brewed up and everybody crowded under a clump of trees for shelter. Suth deliberately took the Moonhawks aside to a sloping boulder where there was just room for all six of them to huddle out of the wet.

Almost at once Dith came striding through the rain, seized Suth by the arm and dragged him out.

"What do you do here?" he snarled. "You stay where we are. Come, all of you."

He hauled Suth across to the trees and in front of everybody flung him to the ground as if he'd been punishing a misbehaving child.

That too was typical. It was another reason why Suth knew he couldn't belong here. He didn't fit in among these people. He was supposed to be the father of a family. Mosu had said so. He had made himself a good digging stick and sharpened its point and hardened it in the fire, as a man was supposed to. He carried it with him wherever he went, but apart from using it to kill a snake, the way his father had shown him, he didn't do any hunting with it. For that you needed to go in a group with the men, and they wouldn't let him, any more than they let him join the game they played under the trees while they were guarding the foragers. Suth wasn't a man. He didn't have the man-scars on his cheeks. So the men made a point of treating him as a child. He hated this.

There were three boys of about Suth's age, but Suth didn't want to play with them. He was supposed to be a man. Besides, they didn't want Suth in their group. It suited them better to copy the men and ignore him.

The eldest of the boys was called Jad. His father was Jun, who was Mosu's eldest son. One evening at the end of the rains, there was a buzz of excitement and the women started to prepare a feast. As they did so they kept picking on Jad, and ordering him about, and scolding him when he hadn't done anything wrong. It was a sort of joke, but at the same time they took it seriously. It mattered.

Suth sat and watched and felt sick in his heart. He understood what this meant. He knew what was going to happen.

When they went down to the lake for

their evening drink, Jad took a fresh leaf and folded it into a shallow bowl. He filled the bowl with water and carried it cupped in his hands back to the cave.

On the way the men ran ahead and set ambushes, and jumped out at him with fierce yells, trying to scare or startle him into spilling the water, but he carried it on steadily.

When they reached the camp, Jad kneeled by the fire and his mother, Fura, scooped ash into the water and mixed it to a thick paste, which Jad then took to where Mosu sat by the cave mouth. He kneeled beside her. She felt for his face, dipped her other hand into the paste and smeared it onto his forehead and cheeks, muttering as she did so. Then Fura took over and covered the rest of his body with paste until he was gray from top to toe.

During this the women preparing the meal didn't gossip and chatter as usual, but sang a slow, wailing chant, too softly for Suth to hear the words. He didn't need to, because the Kin used to do these things in almost exactly the same way. The chant was the song the women sang when one of their children died, because tonight Jad was leaving his mother's side and becoming a man.

Tonight Jad was nobody, neither man nor child, so he sat cross-legged in front of the fire, and ate no food. He was nothing, a gray ghost, and ghosts don't eat. Nor do they sleep among the living, so just before everybody else went into the cave Jun took him along the cliff and helped him to climb a notched pole to a ledge where he could spend the night. Then Jun took the pole away so that Jad would be safe from night hunters.

The next morning he was helped down again, but he wasn't allowed to walk to the lake. Instead the men carried him like a dead body and laid him by the water, where Jun washed the ash from his skin. Then Mosu crouched beside him and cried out in her croaking voice to the power that laired in this place, telling it that from now on Jad was a man.

Jad stood up, and Jun put a pole into his hand and told him to make himself a digging stick, and Dith, who was the best stoneworker in the valley, gave him a new cutter so that he could shape the point.

They all went up the hill to prepare the man feast, laughing and teasing Jad with the very same jokes that the Kin would have used at Suth's own man-making at Odutu below the Mountain.

Suth watched the whole ritual in silence, though his heart was bursting with bitterness and grief. As he had said to Mosu, three moons ago on that second morning in the valley, this should have been his day. At this very moon the Kin would have journeyed to Odutu, and his mother would have smeared the ash onto his body, and his father would have taken him to a particular ledge far up the mountain, to spend the night alone....

It would never happen now. He had no father, no mother. This valley was not the place where a Moonhawk could be made a man.

At the feast he could barely eat. And when the time came for Jad to kneel beside Mosu so that, with Foia guiding her hand, she could slice the first man scar into his cheek, Suth couldn't bear to watch. He closed his eyes and bowed his head. He felt Noli's hand on his arm, but he brushed it away and wept.

―――――

A few days later, on their way back to the cave, the foragers and hunters stopped as usual to inspect the traps they had set. It was almost time to move on to a fresh warren, and only two traps had caught anything. They were Baga's and Tinu's. Dith's had caught nothing. Baga was his sister, and she never missed a chance to tease him.

"You are no hunter, Dith," she called out. "You catch nothing. It takes a woman to build a good trap. See, this girl child makes a better trap than you. See how well it was made."

Dith was furious. He came striding over, kicked the remains of Tinu's trap with his feet, picked up the ground rat and flung it across the hillside.

Tinu flinched as if he'd struck her. Suth gathered her to his side and turned to Dith. He felt his hair starting to bush.

"Baga speaks truth," he snarled. "Tinu builds good traps. You should praise her, not scorn her."

Dith stared at him contemptuously. If a man had spoken to him like that, his hair would have bushed right out, but it didn't even stir.

"Let her build a deer trap," he said. "Then I praise her."

He turned and strutted away.

Several days after that, when they had returned from the morning visit to the lake, Tinu pulled Suth aside.

"Go see deer," she mouthed. "This way. No people. Suth, I ask."

It was a struggle for her to say that much at a time. She looked at him pleadingly and pointed along the slope in the opposite direction to the foraging grounds.

He gestured to Tinu to wait. Noli had already said she was going to forage that day, so he told her that he was going to hunt.

"Be lucky, Suth," she said, just as his mother used to say to his father when he was setting out to look for game.

"You too be lucky, Noli," he answered, as his father would have.

They set off across the rough hillside. It

would have been quicker to take one of the
paths through the scrub, but even the grown
men didn't go there alone. Not all the big
hunting animals slept by day, and one man
by himself was no match for a leopard.

At first, Noli's blessing seemed a strong
one. They'd been walking for a while when
Suth spotted a stoneweed. He marked it
with his mark to gather on the way back and
share with the rest of the Moonhawks. It
was a good sign, he thought as they scrambled on.

The sun was half way up the sky before
they came to a shallow dip running up the
hillside, where a broad strip of coarse grass
had managed to take root. At its lower edge
they found fresh deer tracks coming and
going through gaps in the scrub.

They climbed back up and settled in the
shade of a jut of rock to watch. Time went
by, and more time, and still nothing happened. Suth's restlessness, eased at first by
the change from day after day of foraging,
came back ever more strongly, until he felt
that he could no longer bear to sit still. He
rose to his feet.

"Deer do not come," he said. "We go."

Tinu looked up at him. Her disappointment made it almost impossible for her to speak. Her mouth worked. When the words came he barely understood them.

"I...stay...Suth...I...ask...."

He hesitated and looked around. What harm could come to her here, so far up the open hillside? What except snakes and lizards would be out here in the full heat of the day?

"I go," he said. "When sun is there, I come back."

He pointed a little above the western horizon. She nodded understanding. He picked up his digging stick. Without having thought about it, he knew exactly what he needed to ease his restlessness.

He climbed steadily up the hill, using his digging stick as a staff, ignoring the weight of the sun on his head and shoulders. At last the slope eased, and he could see ahead of him the barrier of jagged boulders that rimmed the bowl. It was farther to them than he had remembered. He looked at the sun. It was more than halfway down. If he went on, they'd be lucky to get back to the cave before dark. He felt obstinate—he would do what he had come to do.

As he turned to continue his climb, his eye was caught by a glimmer above the western ridge, the white peak of a mountain. He recognized it at once. You could see that snow-capped peak from all over the lands which the Kin used to roam, though it might be many days walking away. It was the Mountain above Odutu, the Place of Meeting. When any of the Kin had died, Moonhawk had come in the night and carried their spirit away to the Spirit Place at its summit. And somewhere below was the ledge where Suth would have spent the slow night before the day of becoming a man.

He looked at it and wept for the world that he had lost.

I cannot stay here, he thought as he climbed on. This is not my place.

The Moonhawks had been lucky when they had first crossed the barrier of rocks that crowned the ridge, and had found a way through fairly soon. This time he had to explore some distance along it, trying several openings and finding them blocked, before he recognized the one they had used that first evening.

He would need to know this place, he thought, so he studied the slope below, picking out landmarks, so as to be sure of finding it again. By now it was almost time for him to turn back, but he went stubbornly on, until he reached a place from which he had a clear view of the desert below.

He gazed east. The awful emptiness stretched away and away. It was terrifying, deadly, but still he yearned for it, simply because it was not the prisoning bowl behind him. Here were the huge skies he was used to. Here he could walk day after day after day, and still not reach the end. Soon, soon, in a few more moons, the small ones would be tall and strong enough to do that too, and only Otan would need help. Then he would take them far away to the new Good Places that Bal had dreamed of, and there he would teach them how to live the life they were born to.

Somewhere there must be a way across the desert. He started to study it more delib-

erately, searching for any sign of hope.
Under the clear evening light he could see
for immense distances. The dew trap he and
Noli had found—where was that?... No, it
would be too far to see.... Where had they
climbed the cliff then? A bit to the left?
So...

He stiffened. Something had moved in
that stillness. Not where he happened to be
looking but near enough to catch his eye. It
had come out of the long shade of boulder
into the sun. Where?

There! Two of them...three...moving
one behind the other toward the cliff. Mere
flecks, dark on the yellow gray waste, so far
off that he could see neither heads nor
limbs.

Yet he knew at once what he was looking
at. People. Walking.

Who were they? Nobody ever went down
from the valley into the desert. Some of
Bal's group? The only three who were left
alive? But they didn't move like lost and
starving survivors. There was something
about them that made it seem as if they
knew where they were going....

Yes. He was sure. Whoever they were, there was a way across the desert, and they had found it.

———

By the time Suth had recrossed the ridge, the sun was touching the horizon. It was almost dark before he reached Tinu. She seemed untroubled by his having been gone so long.

She rose as he came and pointed down the slope.

"Suth, I see deer. They come. Go," she mouthed.

He peered down the slope. There was a moon, but it was not more than a quarter full and already well down the western sky. The belt of scrub and the forest were a single dark mass. It was far too dark to tell if the deer that Tinu had seen were still there. When the moon set it would be almost pitch night. There was no hope of their getting back to the cave before then. And soon the big night prowlers would be hunting.

"Too dark," he said. "We find a lair."

He led the way back up the hill.

———

They slept hungry and thirsty, but Suth almost welcomed the discomfort. It was part of the life he knew. Tinu made no complaint. She seemed happy and excited. When Suth woke at first light she was already up, crouching a little way off where a jut of rock gave her a clear view down the hill. As Suth moved to join her she gestured to him to keep low. He crouched beside her and she pointed. Far below them, halfway up the slant of grass, deer were grazing.

Tinu gave a sigh of happiness.

"Men sleep. Deer come," she mumbled. "Deer go. Men come."

Suth grunted. It made sense. The deer had learned to hide from the night prowlers, and to hide again from the daytime hunters. There were just these two times, dawn and dusk, when it was safe for them to graze.

It didn't matter now. It was important for Tinu to be happy, but he was aching to get back to the cave and tell Noli that he now knew that there had to be a way through the desert.

They were in time to see the last of the people disappearing into the scrub on their way to the lake for their morning drink. Hurrying, they caught up as the line wound into the trees. Jun was among the rear guard. He turned, grabbed Suth by the hair, and cuffed him stingingly on the side of the head.

"Where do you go?" he snapped. "This is not good. Do you say you are a man, to come and go?"

He kicked Suth forward. Several of the women scolded him as he made his way up the line to join the Moonhawks.

Noli was clearly relieved to see him.

"Suth, I fear for you," she told him. "The women say you take Tinu, you go away, you leave us. I say you do not do this. But I fear for you."

Suth hardly listened. He took her by the arm.

"Noli," he whispered. "A way goes through the desert. I saw people. They came through the desert."

She didn't react with excited questions, but simply stared at him, frowning, while he explained what he'd seen.

"What people are these?" she asked doubtfully.

Suth had been puzzling about this since he'd woken.

"My thought is this," he said. "They are Moonhawk. They found Good Places beyond the desert. Now Bal sends some back. They say to Fat Pig, and to Little Bat, and all the Kins: *Come to these new Good Places. No murdering strangers are here!*"

Noli frowned and sighed, and then walked on with her head bowed, troubled and silent. When they reached the lake, he drew her aside.

"Why do you not speak?" he asked. "Is it not good, this that I saw?"

She took his hands and looked into his eyes but still didn't answer.

"Does Moonhawk say nothing to you?" he asked.

"Moonhawk does not come to this place," she whispered. "Do not ask more. Oh, Suth, I am sad, sad."

She clutched his hands tight and let go. He could feel her distress, though he didn't understand it. He grunted and moved away. All his excitement was gone, leaving him sour and miserable.

When he glanced back, Noli was standing where he'd left her, staring out across the lake, while the eerie howl of Big Voice floated over the water.

Oldtale

Monkey Is Found Out

Black Antelope grazed far out on the plain.

At evening he lifted up his head and sniffed the air.

He smelled fire.

He smelled the odor of burned flesh.

Thus he thought: *The First Good Place burns. The creatures burn, and An and Ammu and their children.*

He came swiftly, but all was still.

At the sound of his hooves, the creatures came out of their holes and lairs and nests to greet him.

"Who is hurt?" he called to them. "Who burns?"

"None of us," they answered, each one.

In the darkness he saw the glow of a great fire. He heard the sound of singing, and loud boasting.

He came softly to the place and saw An and Ammu and their children feasting around the fire that they had made. His nostrils were filled with the smell of the roast flesh that they ate.

Black Antelope called the First Ones to him.

"Which of you has done this?" he said. "Which of you gave fire to the children of An and Ammu?"

"Not I," said Little Bat.

"Not I," said Fat Pig.

So they answered, each one.

Only Monkey said nothing.

"Was it you, Monkey?" said Black Antelope.

Still Monkey said nothing. But the itchy place under his arm, that had never healed, tickled him.

He scratched.

"Why do you scratch, Monkey?" said Black Antelope.

"A tick bit me," said Monkey.

"Let me breathe on the place and make it well," said Black Antelope.

At that Monkey tried to run away, but Snake caught him and wrapped himself around him so that he could not move, and Black Antelope looked under his arm and saw the place that had not healed.

By that all knew that Monkey had given fire to the children of An and Ammu.

9

Suth began to make plans for their journey. There was no point in waiting for the dry season to be over. Very little rain ever fell in Dry Hills, and clearly none ever did in the desert. (It was some freak of the ground that made little local storms fall over this valley and keep the lake supplied—Suth had decided it was Monkey who made that happen.)

They couldn't carry water, so they would have to find it. The people Suth had seen coming out of the desert must have found water. He wondered if they had been traveling at night not just to avoid the dreadful desert sun. Perhaps there were dew traps they knew about. Dew traps weren't common. There was a good one at Tarutu Rock, and the bad one Suth and Noli had found. Those were the only ones he had seen or heard of. But there might be others in the desert, and better....

And even if they were lucky about water, how would they carry food? In the old Good Places, the Kins used to make straps from the bark of tingin trees, and light nets from special grasses, but he hadn't seen anything like that in the valley. They didn't have gourds. Perhaps they didn't have tingin trees either.

He asked Tinu if she had any ideas and she nodded, gesturing to show she would think about it, but as far as Suth could see, she did nothing.

Besides, she was busy with something else. In all her spare time, at the camp and while they were resting under the trees at midday, she would be shaping grass stems into individual knots, which she stored in a folded leaf and carried around with her. Later she broke branches from the bushes and took them back to the camp.

Then one evening she took Suth aside and led him to a piece of ground she had cleared of loose stuff a little beyond the main camp area. He watched while she laid a lot of twiggy branchlets out on the slope until she had a wide belt of them across the lower half of her cleared patch. There were narrow paths through the belt, running down the slope.

Next she unfolded her leaf and took out the grass knots she had been making. When she laid a line of them out on the rock Suth saw at once what they were. Two grass stems below, twisted together to form a thicker bit, with two more stems sticking out on either side and a round knot at the top. Legs, body, arms, head. People. Tiny grass people.

She showed him some more. These were made in the same way, but each had four stems below a horizontal body that curved up into a neck, and was then pinched over to make the head. Deer.

And now he saw that the slope of rock was the hillside where she'd watched the deer with him, and the line of twigs was the belt of scrub below.

"Clever," he said.

She smiled, and began to move the little grass deer up through the paths to graze on the hillside. She set two little grass men to watch unseen what the deer did. Then more men came to cut branches from the bushes, and block all the paths but one. Halfway down this one they cut a clearing. She showed the deer going in and out through this one path.

Now, while the deer were out on the hillside, the men came creeping back through the scrub. Two groups moved up the hill on either side of the deer, while a smaller one went to the clearing and blocked its lower opening with more branches, and then waited there, ready.

She clapped her hands, and with rapid, deft movements showed the hunters leaping out of ambush.

"Yik-yik-yik-yeek!" she cried. "Wow-wow-waah!"

Suth joined in with the noises of the hunt.

"Oiyu, oiyu, ooiyooo!"

The hunters closed in. The deer fled for the one remaining path and streamed through, only to find themselves trapped in the clearing. Before they could turn back, the hunters from the hillside were on them. All the while Tinu kept up the shrill hoots and squeals that the Kin had used when driving game out of cover toward the hunters. Suth, caught up in the imaginary excitement, joined in.

"Who hunts?" said a man's voice above their heads.

Suth turned and saw Gan and Mohr watching, amused, and no doubt looking for another chance to jeer at him, though they were in fact the least unfriendly of the men.

"Who hunts?" said Mohr again.

"Tinu makes a deer trap," said Suth. "Show, Tinu."

But Tinu was cowering from the men's gaze with her head turned away and her thin arms crossed protectively over her chest. In the end it was Suth who had to show the men what she'd made. At first they laughed and wouldn't take it seriously, but then they got caught up in the excitement, as Suth had been, and called the other men to come over.

It turned out that they weren't nearly as interested in the deer trap as they were in the imaginary hunt. By the time it got too dark to see, they were all crouching around, arguing about it, elbowing each other aside as they tried to have their own way about how the hunt should go. They even chose special grass people to be themselves, so that they could play the most important part, and then boasted about what they'd done as if it had really happened, and quarreled with each other about their share in the hunt. None of them paid any attention to Tinu. The model was their game, their toy.

In the end they spoiled it, moving the cunning little grass models roughly around until they lost their shapes, and scattering the belt of twigs apart. They were still arguing about it as they built the wall across the mouth of the cave.

Over the next few days, the men came to Suth one after the other, and either asked or ordered him to tell Tinu to make them their own little grass man, and grass deer for the man to hunt. Tinu seemed happy to do it, and to replace them when they were spoiled, and to rebuild her model of the hillside so that they could play their game afresh each evening. They ignored Tinu, sitting to one side, deftly knotting men and deer for them out of grass stems, and listening to what they said.

And then, suddenly, one evening, it was all decided. They would start to build a real deer trap the next day. Tinu listened with dismay.

"This not good," she told Suth in her mumbling whisper. "First men wait. Watch deer. Deer come, go. Men watch."

She was right, of course. Somebody had to go and watch the deer in the early dawn, to see how they came and went through the paths in the scrub, or the men would build their trap in the wrong place.

"Tinu, I cannot say this to them," he told her. "To them I am a child. They do not hear me."

She hesitated, then bent her head and fluttered her fingers in the air.

"Suth, I ask," she mouthed. "You, me, go. Go now. See deer, sun up."

He looked around. The notion of sleeping out under the stars again was very tempting. It was almost dark, but the men were still arguing about their game. The women were on the far side of the fire. Suth walked quietly over to where Noli was sitting among the small ones. Po and Otan were already asleep, and Mana almost.

"I go with Tinu," he whispered. "We watch deer."

"This makes the men angry," she said.

"Is Dith my father, to say yes and no to me?"

"When you are gone, I tell them."

"My thanks."

He went back to Tinu and squatted down beside her. When no one was looking in their direction, they rose and moved away.

⸻

They laired well up on the hill, as before, and in the earliest dawn made their way down the slope, moving carefully, not dislodging a pebble, and bending low so that they were hidden from anything in the dip of ground. Then they turned and crept toward the rim of the dip.

The deer were there. Suth counted them. Ten and three more, in a rough line, working their way up the slope. Most were nosing among the rough clumps of grass, but at any moment two or three had their heads up, alert, with ears cupped to catch the slightest sound.

Suth and Tinu watched them in silence. The light grew stronger. Then Tinu touched his arm and signaled him back. As soon as the deer were hidden she put her mouth to his ear.

"Make deer run," she whispered. "This way."

She gestured to show what she wanted. He nodded. It made sense. This was their one chance to see which path the deer naturally used for escape if they were startled on the hillside. He would need to hurry though. Soon it would be full day and the deer would be going back under cover until dusk. He climbed as fast and silently as he could, wormed his way across the open hillside above the dip, using any cover the boulders gave him, then down again in a crouching lope, below where Tinu waited.

When he crawled to the rim of the dip, the deer were still there, apparently undisturbed, but to judge by their fidgety movements just getting ready to return to shelter. He gave himself a moment to catch his breath and then jumped to his feet, yelling and waving his digging stick.

Instantly they were streaking down the slope, clearing the boulders with great flowing bounds. They swerved away as he sprinted to head them off, but Tinu herself had come farther down and rose whooping to meet them. They swung back, heading for three separate pathways as the herd split apart. They were well ahead of him now. There was no hope of his cutting them off.

Then, just as the nearest group reached the scrub, something leaped to meet it, bowling the leading deer clean over. The others vanished, but that one lay thrashing and struggling to rise while the leopard that had been waiting in ambush wrenched snarling at its neck.

Suth halted, panting, and raised his digging stick. The movement caught the leopard's eye. It looked up and stared at him. Its tail lashed to and fro and it bared its fangs, but it stayed where it was, crouched over the deer.

Suth hesitated. If I can drive it off, he thought, I can drag the deer home, and then even Dith will have to give me praise.

Though he knew he was doing a stupid and dangerous thing, he took a pace forward, just to see.

Instantly the leopard was springing for his throat.

His heart clenched in his chest, but his arm and his body answered without thought, lunging full strength to meet the attack. He was belted sideways. His digging stick was torn from his grasp. There was a searing pain down his left arm. He was falling, helpless. A hard thing crashed against his skull. Blackness.

He woke to the throb of pain, pain all through him.

A voice mouthing his name.

"Suth! Suth!"

Tinu.

He opened his eyes. Through the pain

haze, he saw her face, close above his. The haze half cleared. He wiped the rest away with the back of his right hand. It was blood. The pain found its sources, aching fiercely at the side of his head, searing down his left arm from the shoulder. He craned, and saw his left side smeared with blood from deep gouges slashed down the arm. He eased himself up, clutching the wound with his right hand, trying to stem the flow.

The leopard! His body sprang alert. He stared around. No sign. But a sound, a ghastly retching cough, mixed with violent thrashings among the bushes.

"Run, Tinu! Run!" he gasped, and staggered to his feet, searching for his digging stick.

Gone.

A rock, then...

His eye fell on the body of the deer.

He forgot the wound, forgot the pain. This was what he had fought for. He seized it by the hind legs and frenziedly started to drag it up the hill.

It was too heavy for him. The pain came rasping back. He stopped and stood, shuddering, with the blood welling from the wound. He looked back. Still no sign of the leopard, though the racket in the bushes rose and fell. He bent and dragged the body a few more paces toward a scatter of loose rocks and began to pile them over it. Every few seconds he glanced down the slope, but nothing came.

The daze returned, but he worked on. Tinu was helping him. When the body was covered he stood swaying. The valley seemed full of darkness.

"Face hurt, Suth," said Tinu's voice.

He put his fingers to his left cheek and flinched at his own touch. Another wound, but his hands were so covered with blood that he couldn't tell how bad it was.

"You die, Suth?"

The darkness cleared and he stood erect.

"No, I live," he said.

He must tell the men himself that he had fought a leopard and robbed it of its prey. Their faces would change. He must see that.

He was in no state to scramble across rocks, so despite the danger he headed down toward the scrub, where the going was less rough. The sun was above the ridge now, and warmed his back. He walked slowly, but steadily at first, clutching his right hand over his wounded arm. The flow of blood seemed to ease.

But then the darkness closed in again, filling his eyesight and his mind, though his legs still walked as they did in dreams. There were clear patches in the darkness, when he would find Tinu holding his elbow and guiding him carefully along, and he'd remember where he was and what had happened, and then there'd be nothing but pain and darkness once more.

They stopped, and then they seemed to be climbing. Tinu's voice told him to sit and she eased him down onto a rock. She was gone.

He waited, and then she was back and coaxing his head up and putting something against his mouth. The smell woke him.

Stoneweed.

He sipped, and his mind cleared. She'd remembered the stoneweed he'd marked a few days earlier, and then forgotten to gather on his way back to the cave, in his eagerness to tell Noli what he'd seen. Tinu had fetched it for him.

"My thanks," he muttered, and sipped again, carefully, feeling the warmth and strength running through his veins. He passed her the stoneweed and she took a couple of sips and handed it back.

He saw her stiffen and gaze down the slope. She let out a shout, climbed a boulder, and waved and shouted again. Suth rose, swaying, and saw men with digging sticks halted just above the scrub and gazing toward them. *They have come to find me*, he thought. *Noli told them I watched deer. They are angry.* Then he thought, *No, they are too many. They go to build their trap.*

He swayed and almost fell, but managed to settle onto a boulder. Two of the men were climbing the slope. His eyesight was all blurred, but from the way they walked he recognized them as Mohr and Gan. He rose. He was almost too weak to stand, but he knew what he needed to say and do.

He held out the stoneweed to them, one-handed, the gesture of a man offering a gift to another man, an equal.

"Mohr, Gan," he said. "I fought with a leopard. It killed a deer. I drove it off. The deer is under rocks. Tinu shows you."

"You are hurt," said Mohr. "We must take you to Mosu, to see to your hurts."

"No, I wait here. You bring the deer. I, Suth, ask this. Here is my gift. Drink."

Gan accepted the stoneweed, took a couple of sips and passed it to Mohr, who did the same and then handed it back.

Suth sat and closed his eyes. He heard the men muttering to each other, questioning Tinu, Tinu painfully mouthing her answer, for once not afraid to speak to them. All three moved away. He heard other voices from farther down the slope. They faded.

While Suth waited, he did his best to clean the wounds in his arm and cheek, using spit from his mouth. The three claw slashes on his arm were deep and throbbing, though the stoneweed dulled the pain. The cut on his cheek seemed shallower. Perhaps his head had flinched just in time from the strike.

He eased the torn flesh together with his

fingertips, as best he could. *I will wear these marks for all my days*, he thought. *All will know how I fought the leopard.*

He finished the stoneweed. He'd never before had so much all to himself, and the juice made him drowsy. He lay down on the hillside and fell asleep.

A voice woke him. Tinu again, urgent, excited.

"Suth! Suth! Wake! You kill...leopard! See! Gan bring!"

The words were bursting from her. He could barely make them out. Blearily he sat up and looked. Men were coming up the slope, two of them with loads over their shoulder. He rose. They stopped a few paces away and stood looking at him. Their faces had changed.

"Suth," said Mohr stiffly. "You killed the leopard. We found it among the scrub. Your digging stick is fast in its throat. So it died. I, Mohr, praise."

"I, Gan, also praise," said Gan. "I bring your brave digging stick. See, it is here."

He held it out, but froze as Suth, without thought, wiped the back of his hand across his bleeding cheek before stepping forward to take it.

"See, Mohr!" whispered Gan. "Suth's face! He has the man-scar! The leopard made it!"

Oldtale

How People Hunted Black Antelope

Such was their lust for roast flesh that the children of An and Ammu would eat nothing else. They passed by the seeded grasses and did not gather them. They left ripe berries on the bushes, and fruits on the vines, and nuts on the ground beneath the trees, as if they had been dirt. All day from sun up they hunted and killed the creatures, and at sundown they made a fire and roasted their catch and ate until their stomachs were round and full, like a ripe gourd. They fell sick, but they did not care.

The creatures came to Black Antelope. They said, "The people hunt and kill us day after day, without rest. Tens and tens and tens of us they kill for their feasts. Soon none of us are left."

Black Antelope gathered the First Ones. He said, "The people are spoiling this Good Place that we made for ourselves. Go, each of you, far away from here, and make new Places for the people to live. Set them apart. Then the people must journey between them. See to it that there is food of all kinds, a little of each kind. Then the people must forage as well as hunt, and not fall sick from eating only flesh. See to it that each Place has its season. Then the people will leave it for a while, and the creatures can breed and the plants can grow and seed, and all will be well."

The First Ones agreed, and did all that.

Then Black Antelope took the shape of a common antelope and let himself be seen by the children of An and Ammu as they were setting off to hunt. They saw him grazing on the plain a little way off.

Datta said, "We hunt that antelope."

The others were afraid. They said, "Do we kill and eat antelope? Is not Black Antelope the greatest of the First Ones?"

Da said, "Why do we not eat it? Which of us is of the Kin of Black Antelope?"

Datta said, "See how fat he is. His flesh is very good to eat."

But still the others were afraid.

Da and Datta said, "We are the best. You must do as we say. You swore it at Odutu below the Mountain."

Because they had sworn at Odutu, they agreed to hunt the antelope.

Black Antelope saw them creeping toward him and moved a little away and grazed again. They crept further, and again he moved away, and again, and again. All day he did this, and always they said in their hearts: "Next time we have him." The thought of fat roast flesh was strong in their mouths.

At sunset he led them to a water hole where there was blueroot growing beside the water. They drank, and dug out the blueroot and ate them, and said, "Tomorrow we return to the First Good Place and hunt there."

Next day they woke and saw Black Antelope grazing close by, and again they hunted him all day, and at sunset he led them to a water hole where there were binjas growing beside the water. They drank, and gathered and husked the binja seed and ate it, and said, "Tomorrow we return to the First Good Place and hunt there."

So it was for many, many days. And at last they came to one of the new Good Places, which the First Ones had made for them, and there Black Antelope left them. As he passed by the water holes on his way, he drank them dry. And he ate the binjas and the blueroot and everything else that grew near them, so that the children of An and Ammu should never return to the First Good Place.

10

On Mosu's instructions Foia licked Suth's wounds clean and pounded leaves of bitter bush and pressed them on. The juices stung like fire but dried the exposed flesh so that the blood stopped oozing and scabs began to form. Mohr and Gan carried the news out to the foragers and hunters, who came home early for the feast. The men butchered and roasted the deer.

Suth knew very little of all this. He was weak with loss of blood and groggy with shock and the after effects of the stoneweed. He was aware of a moment when the Moonhawks were suddenly there, and Noli's concern for him, and Po's wide-eyed awe at his wound, and Mana settling beside him to be hugged by his good arm.

The men came too, and spoke to him in new voices. He couldn't see their faces clearly, or understand the words, but he knew that they were praise. Dith was among them, who had scorned him so. He too spoke praise.

Now I may die, Suth thought, overwhelmed with happiness despite the pain.

He would have slept where he was, in the full sun and on bare rock, but the Moonhawks gathered bedding for him inside the mouth of the cave and Noli helped him to his feet and led him there to sleep in the shade.

They woke him for the feast. He was still too weak and dazed to do his part unaided, so Mohr held his hand on the cutter and helped him slice open the belly of the leopard and draw out the heart and liver and cut them in pieces, so that everybody could eat of them and the power of the leopard would be in them all.

Night fell and there was firelight and singing and many mouths speaking praise. Somebody came and put something hard and round into his hand. It was a cutter.

The giver was Dith. He had done the same for Jad at his man-making.

Suth managed to speak his thanks, but when he was called on to make his boast he needed to be helped to his feet and then could only stand there, mumbling. He knew what he wanted to say, but the words wouldn't come to his mouth. But no one mocked him, for no one—not even Mosu, who had seen everything and knew everything—had heard of anybody who had fought and killed a leopard alone.

For the next several days Suth was too feeble to do more than make the morning and evening trips to the lake, so Noli took the Moonhawks foraging, while he rested at the camp.

When he was strong enough to join them, she continued to come with them and he began to feel that things were back now as they should be, with his family together and whole, and given their place and respected by the men and women of the valley. The men were busy building deer traps, and he might have joined them, or sat with them in the shade and played their game with them, and they wouldn't have made him unwelcome, but he preferred to be with the Moonhawks and plan for the day they would leave.

Then Mosu fell ill, and became too weak to hobble to the lake, and in too much pain to be carried there by the men. Instead the women folded leaves into bowls, which they filled with water and carried carefully back to her between their two cupped hands. Though Foia was there to look after her, Noli said she must stay with her too, and even when Mosu got better and could go to the lake again she continued to stay.

Suth didn't like this at all. He resented it much more than he had before, and resented how silent and withdrawn Noli had become. One evening he could bear it no more. After they had finished eating, he took her aside.

"Why do you do this?" he said. "I, Suth, ask. Why do you not speak? Why do you choose to be with the old woman always? You are Moonhawk. Your place is with us."

She shook her head, and he thought she was going to tell him again that her reasons were secret—dream stuff that she could share only with Mosu. But for a while she simply sat with her head bowed, staring at her folded hands. When she did speak it was in an almost toneless mutter, slow and hesitant.

"I tell you," she said. "Words are not good for this, Suth. But see."

She picked up a small rock.

"I say *Rock*, Suth," she said. "I see the rock. You see it. You say the word. We see the same. We say the same. Rock."

"Rock?" said Suth, puzzled.

"Rock," she said again, and put it into his hand, closing his fingers around it.

"I say *Moonhawk*," she said. "What do you see, Suth?"

He frowned.

"I see…a great bird?" he said hesitantly.

"Where is this bird, Suth?"

"Where?…In my head, I think. It is like when I remember. Like when I say *Sometimes River*. Then I see the river in my head."

"Only this, Suth? No more? I tell you now how Moonhawk comes to me. It is night—

dark, dark. No moon. No stars. But she is there. Moonhawk. There is a yellow eye. There are wings.... I do not *see* them, Suth. They are there. I have no word for this. And I am small. She is big, big. I am afraid, yes. But my heart is happy. This is how Moonhawk comes."

Suth looked at the rock in his hand. He tightened his fingers around it, feeling its hardness. What Noli was telling him—trying to tell him—was not like that at all. There seemed to be no place for it in his mind.

"You do not see the thing I see?" Noli suggested.

"Noli, I cannot see this," he said.

"Mosu sees the thing I see," said Noli. "She lives long, long. Many times her spirit goes from her body. It journeys where the First Ones are. They speak to her spirit, wonderful things. All this she tells me. Mosu knows how it is when Moonhawk comes to me."

"Moonhawk comes to Mosu?" said Suth, more puzzled than ever.

Noli shook her head, hesitated and sighed.

"Moonhawk does not come to this place," she said sadly. "He is too strong, Big Voice."

He grabbed her wrist, appalled.

"Moonhawk came!" he exclaimed. "She spoke in your dream! *Monkey is sick!* She said this to you!"

She eased his fingers away.

"She does not come again," she muttered. "Big Voice is strong in this place, too strong."

She paused. He thought she had finished.

"Suth," she said. "Mosu says this to me: *Big Voice comes to none of my people. They are sick. Now, soon, I die. Then he comes to you, Noli.*"

Now he understood what she had been trying to tell him.

"And you do this thing, Noli?" he said.

"No. You are Moonhawk. I, Suth, say this."

She wouldn't look at him. She was ashamed. She was betraying him, and the others, betraying all the dead generations of Moonhawk. He could feel her shame.

"What is Monkey to you?" he insisted. "We are Moonhawk. Soon, Noli, soon we leave this place. When the moon is big, we go. I saw people in the desert. I told you this. They know a way through the desert. We find that way. We take food, we find water. We cross the desert and find our Kin. We go far from this place. Then Moonhawk comes to you again. I am the father, Noli. You are the mother. We are Moonhawk. I, Suth, say this!"

Still she didn't look at him. His eye was caught by a small figure, tottering up the slope, black against the firelight.

"See, Noli!" he said. "Otan! In the desert Moonhawk came. She said to you: *Go back. Leave Bal and the others. Find Otan. I show you water. Take Otan there.* Do you say, *Otan is not Moonhawk?* Do you say, *Here he is Monkey?*"

She looked up and he saw the firelight glinting off her tears.

"Big Voice is strong, Suth," she whispered. "When he comes, I am small. He is big, big. I am afraid. My heart is sad."

Suth lay sleepless in the reeking dark of the cave, thinking about Noli. He was full of anger toward her, though at the same time he was aware of her misery. He was angry with Mosu too, for taking Noli away from the Moonhawks where she belonged. And he was angrier still with Monkey, though he knew how dangerous it was to have such feelings about a First One.

Why didn't Moonhawk help? Why didn't she come to Noli any more? Was she too afraid of Monkey? That must be it.

The mood of his anger changed at the thought. If Monkey was too strong for Moonhawk, then no wonder he was too strong for Noli. That was why she was so miserable. She knew in her heart she was Moonhawk, and that she wanted what Suth wanted, to leave this valley and journey and find the rest of the Kin and be with them and live the old life in the way that they knew. But Monkey and Mosu were keeping her here.

He didn't know how they did this. All he knew was that Monkey was one of the First Ones, and had great power, and Mosu had some of that power because she had served Monkey so long.

A moment later something brushed

against his hip. Fingers moved up his side and found his hand, and held it.

Noli.

She too had been lying sleepless in the dark, and had heard his sigh, and had reached out.

This is good, he thought. I am the father and she is the mother and we are Moonhawk still. Noli knows this. Now I see what I must do. I must make ready for our journey. The small ones are strong with the good food they have eaten in this place. When all is ready I will say to Noli, *Now we go to find the Kin—Suth, Tinu, Po, and Mana. Do you come? Do you stay? And Otan. Does he come? Does he stay?* Then for Otan's sake she will come, because he is Moonhawk.

There were things he must do. The next morning, on their way back from the lake, he told Noli. "Today I watch deer. Tinu comes."

Noli looked at him, started to speak, and stopped, then smiled.

"Fight no leopard, Suth," she said.

He laughed and she joined him.

Yes, he thought. Whatever Monkey tells her, she will come with me when I go.

He set off with Tinu. Since his fight with the leopard he had been allowed to come and go very much as he pleased, though he was sure that if he'd tried to take all the Moonhawks with him he would still have been stopped. But nobody seemed to mind if he went off with just Tinu.

This time they didn't go as far as the area where the deer grazed, but stopped below the place at which the Moonhawks had first entered the valley. He knew it by the rat warren he had seen.

"We store food," he told Tinu. "Food for many days. You make a place where we keep it. Tinu, this is secret."

She nodded and searched around, eventually choosing a place where a huge single flat rock had split in two, leaving a deep crack about as wide as a spread hand. She then collected rocks and began to wedge them down into the crack to form the floor of her food store.

Suth left her to it and went to look for lizards. It was still early enough for them to be out, basking away the night chill, and he caught two, slit them open with the cutter and set them to dry in the sun. Well-dried lizard would keep for many days. The Kin had always carried some on their longer journeys. To chew it was like chewing the bark of a tree, but slowly the good juices were released and could be swallowed.

The sun climbed, baking the hillside, and the lizards slid back under rocks. A rat bobbed up at the warren. No point in setting traps yet. Rat meat was too juicy to dry well. Tinu could set some a day or two before they left. He made his way down and cautiously ventured among the scrub, pausing and peering around every few paces. Deep in under a thorny bush, he spotted a yellow bracket fungus of a kind he knew. It tasted of nothing, and had not much goodness in it, but it was plant food and it didn't rot, so he began to work his way around the bush looking for somewhere to wriggle in under the fierce thorns.

Kneeling at a possible gap he found himself face-to-face with a dark gray snake, as long as his arm, gliding toward him.

It stopped and reared its head, jaws wide.

He froze. His right hand tightened on his digging stick and raised it slowly toward his shoulder. *Do not attack*, his father had told him. *Soon it turns away. Strike then.*

It turned, and he struck, jabbing at the base of the head, but the tangle of twigs spoiled his aim and he caught it farther along the body, where it was too thick for the spine to be broken with a single blow.

Instantly it lashed around. He flung his weight on the stick, pinning the body fast, and then, still bearing down, rolled the stick along the thrashing body until he had it safely held behind the head. Now he could reach in, work his fingers under the stick and grasp the snake behind the jaws, so that it couldn't turn and bite. He dragged it out, laid the head on the ground and pounded it with the butt of his stick until it was dead.

He rose, panting. His head, arms and shoulders were bloody from wrestling in under the thorns, but he didn't care. This was how, many moons ago, watched by his father, he had killed his first snake. It was a good sign. Snake flesh dried well and was better to eat than lizard.

He carried the body up to where Tinu was

working and slit it into strips with the cutter, set them to dry beside the lizards, and went to see how she was getting on.

She had made a good-sized hollow and was wedging the cracks with pebbles, but when Suth appeared she stopped work, laid a flat rock over the top, and scattered a few smaller ones on top of it, so that it looked like just a pile of loose stuff that happened to have jammed into the crack.

"This is good, Tinu," he said.

She smiled, pleased, and didn't try to hide her face.

While she finished what she was doing, he went and turned the lizards over, then found a patch of shade and rested, staring out over the forest and brooding over the question of leaving the valley. Not this next big moon—he wouldn't be ready. The one after. Till then, forage for extra food. All the families kept spare supplies—they would ask no questions. Every second day, bring some of it out to put in the food store Tinu was building. Set the meat he had caught to continue drying. Tinu could guard it from scavengers while he hunted for more....

Then the biggest problem—how to sneak

all the Moonhawks away, to get far enough ahead for them not to be hunted down....

The ground trembled, and with it the rock against which he was leaning. He was so used by now to these quakings that he would barely have noticed, but before the shock was over he heard Tinu cry out.

He looked up and saw her backing away with her mouth open and her arms half raised in fear or astonishment.

Snake! he thought.

He snatched up his stick and ran. She saw him coming and pointed to the crack in the rock.

Her food store had disappeared.

He frowned, bewildered.

"Rock…break…!" Tinu gasped.

Now he saw that the crack was wider than it had been before, almost twice as wide. He peered in, expecting to see the rocks Tinu had used lodged farther down, but no. The cleft had no bottom. It was part of a crack in the hillside, and went right down into blackness. Out of it rose, stronger than he'd ever smelled it, the strange reek that always hung over the lake and wafted to and fro across the valley.

He backed away and looked around. Nothing seemed to have changed. The sun was high, and beneath it the immense bowl lay green and still. Then, down in the forest, a Big Voice called, and another answered, and another and another, until the steamy air rang with their wild voices.

Slowly the clamor died into silence.

Suth frowned again.

This didn't happen.

Big Voice called in the morning, and again in the evening, one first and then the next, waiting for each other to finish before they replied. Sometimes one or two might call in the rest of the day. But never like this.

Never with one mad voice together in the heat of noon.

Oldtale

The Choosing of Mates

When An and Ammu saw that all their children had gone from them, they said, "Our time is over," and they went into the desert and lay down, and their spirits left their bodies and wandered through the desert, mourning for their lost children.

The First Ones heard their groanings and weepings, and went and carried them up the Mountain above Odutu. They gave them stoneweed to drink, so that they might forget their sorrow.

As they drank they spat the

seeds down the mountain. The seeds fell in the desert, where they grow to this day.

Thus An and Ammu forgot their sorrow.

But their children foraged and hunted in the new Good Places that the First Ones had made for them, and learned their paths and their seasons, and their water holes and dew traps and lairs. So they grew to be men and women.

Then Nal, who was of the Kin of Moonhawk, met with Turka, who was of the Kin of Little Bat, by the salt pan beyond Lusan-of-the-Ants.

Turka said, "Now I ask the blessing of Little Bat to leave her Kin, and be your mate, and become of the Kin of Moonhawk."

Nal said, "This is my thought also."

They took salt from the pan and mixed it with spittle and smeared it on each other's forehead, to show that they were now chosen.

Datta came to Nal and said, "Why is there salt on your forehead? Who has chosen you before I have made my choice? I must have first choice of the men. I am the best, as you swore at Odutu below the Mountain."

Nal said, "Not so. Two must make choice of mates, each choosing the other. I do not choose you, Datta. You are too proud for a mate. I choose Turka."

Datta went to Da and said, "Nal chose Turka for his mate before you took your choice of the women. You are wronged by him, as I am by Turka."

Da was angry. He called the children of An and Ammu to meet him beside Sometimes River, and said, "We are wronged. Nal and Turka chose each other for mates before we took our choice. We must choose first. We are the best, as you swore at Odutu below the Mountain."

The others had no answer, because they had sworn as he said.

Now Crocodile was lying in wait in the river. She heard what was said, and she put a thought into Celda's mind, who was of her Kin.

Celda whispered with the other women.

They said, "Choose, then, Da. Then all choose after you. Which of us women do you choose for your mate?"

Da looked at them all, carefully.

He said, "I choose Preela."

Preela answered him, "I do not choose you, Da. You are too proud for a mate."

Then Da chose among the others, each in turn, and they answered him in the same way, as they had agreed. And when Datta chose among the men, so did they, until there were none left to choose but Datta and Da themselves.

They looked at each other, and Da said, "Datta, I do not choose you. You are too proud for a mate."

And so said Datta to Da.

Then the others chose among themselves until all had mates, and they were satisfied. Only Da and Datta had none. So to this day there are eight Kins only and Monkey has no Kin.

11

When Suth and Tinu got back to the camp
they found a commotion. All those who
were there were gathered by the mouth of
the cave, and as others came hurrying in
they joined the circle.

Suth wormed his way through and saw
that something had happened to Mosu. She
wasn't sitting in her usual place, but was
lying on her back on a pile of bedding just
inside the mouth of the cave. Foia was
kneeling, rubbing her feet and calves.

Mosu gasped and twitched. Her mouth
worked convulsively, but the sounds she
made weren't words. The people watched in
silence for a while, but then moved apart
and talked in low voices.

Suth and Tinu set off to meet the returning foragers, but the news had reached them too and they were almost home. Suth found Noli and told her what he had seen.

"I think she dies," he said.

"She said this," said Noli. "Big Voice also. He shook the place, and spoke. This noon he did it. I told Paro and the women. They also had heard him speak. They did not understand his speaking, and they would not hear me. Gora came from the camp, and then they knew I told truth."

She spoke gravely but vaguely, as if she was thinking of something else. Suth frowned. He didn't at all like her being able to understand what that wild calling in the forest had meant, when no one else could. Nor did he like Paro and the others knowing that she could do this. Now that the time was so near when he was going to try to sneak the Moonhawks away, he didn't want anyone paying special attention to Noli. But he said nothing.

When they reached the cave they found Mosu was not yet dead, and she was still alive that night when they went into the cave, so they carried her in with them and laid her in her usual place. The next morning she was no better and no worse, so they propped her outside the cave and Foia fed her chewings as if she'd been weaning a child, and spat water into her mouth from cupped leaves, which the women had carried up from the lake.

For ten days and ten more Mosu didn't die. The moon grew to its biggest and back to its smallest and started to grow again. Suth saw little of Noli. They took turns foraging, and even when they were both at the camp she spent all her time with Mosu, rubbing her limbs, cleaning her, or just sitting beside her and holding her twitching hand. When she went down to the lake with the Moonhawks, she moved in a kind of dream, not seeing or hearing anything, dealing with Otan's needs automatically, leaving everything else to Suth.

He hated and resented this, and he only didn't yell at her and perhaps even strike her because he could see that she was miserable too.

On the days when Suth foraged he gathered as much as he could, and saw to it that the others did the same, and on the days when Noli went, he and Tinu carried the surplus out to hide in the new food store that Tinu had built. Once there he hunted. He caught and dried several more lizards, and found a juiceroot in the scrub and marked it with his mark.

Meanwhile Tinu guarded their drying meat from vultures and worked steadily at the task Suth had given her, of finding some way of carrying food other than in their hands, as they would have the cliff to climb down. Tinu found how to fold the big leaves to make a sort of bag, which she fastened with a twist of braided grass. She then made a longer twist, braided and rebraided, and tied several bags along its length. They could be carried like that slung around a neck or hung over a shoulder. The bags, though, were fragile, and it took her all day to find the right grass stems and braid them into a single length. She had finished two lengths, and made and filled the bags and tied them on, by the time Mosu finally died.

They woke in the morning and found her spirit gone. They propped her body in its usual place by the mouth of the cave and piled rocks around it to keep it safe while they went down to the lake. Foia and a few of the elders stayed at the camp, while the rest went foraging.

Suth had thought that Noli would want to stay behind, but she joined the foragers and worked in a kind of daze, not hearing, not speaking, as if her spirit was far away— wherever Mosu's spirit had gone, perhaps. Everyone else was silent and troubled. The men didn't hunt, but worked quietly alongside the women. There was none of the usual chat, and when they rested, the men didn't play their game.

Before they started work again, a porcupine came scuttling past, climbing the open hillside in the full heat of the day. This was not a thing that happened. Porcupines are night animals, and in any case keep to dense scrub. Three of the men leaped on it and beat it to death with their digging sticks, but with none of the cries and boastings that usually went with a good kill.

Hardly had they finished when another one came past. That too was killed and brought in. Then a group of deer nosed out of the scrub, and another one farther off, and another one, not stopping to graze but pausing every now and then to gaze anxiously around, and then trotting on. There was no point in trying to hunt them when they were as alert as that, so the people simply watched them go, but with steadily growing unease.

Without much discussion they decided not to forage that afternoon, and made their way back to the camp to prepare the death feast for Mosu. As they wound their way in a silent line through the scattered scrub of the foraging grounds, Big Voice started to howl, one far off, and another nearer by, and another to the right, and more and more, their wavering hoots rising and falling and floating away across the hot, still valley.

Suth looked at Noli. He'd noticed one or two of the others watching her, as if they'd expected something from her, but she'd stayed completely withdrawn, wrapped in her own thoughts.

"He sings for Mosu?" he suggested.

For once she seemed to hear him, and answered, frowning.

"I do not know," she muttered. "I hear no words in his singing. He sings only."

Back at the cave, though it was only midafternoon, they built up the fire and set the porcupines to roast and trooped down to the lake. Normally at this time of day the forest was still, but now the whooping of Big Voice went on and on, untiring, and flocks of birds rose from the treetops and flew to and fro, and then, instead of settling back among the branches, gathered and rose higher and headed away toward the south.

Then, when they were in among the denser scrub, the leading men came face-to-face with a leopard and two half-grown cubs, padding along the path toward them. The men raised their digging sticks. The leopard hissed, backed off, and slipped away under the bushes with the cubs gliding behind it.

Warily they trooped past the place where the leopards had disappeared, but nothing happened. Suth, near the end of the party, looked back over his shoulder and saw that as soon as the people were gone the three animals had come back onto the path and were gliding away up the hill. It was very strange. What were they doing? Where were they going?

Nothing was stirring under the trees, but the cries of Big Voice rang all around them. When they drank at the lake, the water was very warm.

They returned to the cave, many of the women carrying leaf bowls of water. The men unpiled the rocks from around Mosu's body, and the women poured the water over her, weeping as they did so. Her first son, Jun, cut a leg from a porcupine and laid it in her lap, and the chief women brought offerings of nuts and seed paste.

They ate a little, and then Jun stood and wept praise. In a quiet voice, with many pauses, he spoke of Mosu's wisdom, and the power of her dreams, and named her children and their children one by one.

As the sun went down the women formed two lines for the death dance to help Mosu's spirit on its way. They did it differently from the Kin, who danced where they stood, with stamping and clapping. Here the two lines moved together and apart with shrilling, wavering cries, while the men clapped the rhythm and made deep groaning noises through closed lips.

The Moonhawks watched, sitting a little to one side, until Noli, who had so far sat with dry, staring eyes, heaved herself convulsively to her feet and cried, in a huge voice that was not her own, "He is gone! Big Voice is gone!"

The dance stopped. Heads turned. In the silence they heard that the forest was silent too. The howling of Big Voice, which had filled the valley all afternoon, was still. Even the clatter of the parrots settling into their nests for the night was missing. Not a bird twittered.

They looked at each other, and back to Noli.

She raised both arms, shuddering, and then stretched one out and pointed.

"See!" she croaked. "They go!"

They turned and looked. A little way off, but clearly visible in the half-light of dusk, a few spindly shapes were scrambling rapidly toward the ridge. They had thin, angular limbs and long tails, which they carried

curled over their short bodies. Their heads
were small and round. They went on all
fours but used their front limbs more like
arms than legs as they scrambled over the
tumbled rocks.

The watchers knew at once what they
were seeing, though few of them had ever
caught more than a glimpse of one of these
creatures in its home, high in the dense
canopy of leaves.

"He goes!" they whispered. "Big Voice
goes!"

They danced no more that night. Many
wanted to copy the animals and leave at
once, but the thought of lairing out in the
open was too alarming, so in the end they
carried Mosu into the cave and walled
themselves in, as they had done every other
night of their lives.

Suth had to take Noli by the elbow and
guide her in, as she seemed not to know
where she was or what she was doing, and
when he pushed her down into her place
she fell at once into a deep, slow-breathing
sleep. Everyone else seemed restless with
unease. Even the small ones picked up the

general feeling and whimpered or cried, but they all slept in the end.

They were woken by screams. A harsh, croaking yell.

"Fire!" it cried. "Out! Out! Go! Fire comes!"

Suth jerked up. The yelling voice was close above him. Somebody, something was moving between him and the pale patch of sky above the wall. He reached out. Noli was not in her place. His searching hand touched flesh, a leg. It shuddered violently. The clamor began again.

"Fire! I see fire! It comes! Out! Go!"

Noli.

He stood and grappled her to him. Her body jerked and thrashed, like the body of a snake after its back is broken but before it is truly dead. Otan yelled with terror. The cave was full of shouting.

Suth was a lot stronger than Noli, but tonight trying to hold her was like wrestling with a trapped animal. She wrenched herself free. He followed, trying to get a fresh hold on her, as she struggled to the mouth of the cave and started to tear at the wall.

"Out!" she screamed. "Fire comes!

Moonhawk is here! She says, Go! Out! Fire!"

A man grabbed and held her.

"Witch dream," he grunted as she struggled and bit.

Suth seized the man's forearm and tried to wrench it from its hold.

"No!" he shouted. "This dream is true! Monkey is gone! Now Moonhawk comes! Moonhawk sends true dreams to Noli! I, Suth, say this!"

The man didn't seem to understand. Suth turned and heaved a rock down from the wall, but already others, filled with panic by Noli's cries, were pulling it apart. In another few moments they were crowding out into the huge night silence. There was nothing but sky, and the moonlit forest, and the far, dark ridges of the valley.

Then the ground trembled. A long, hoarse sigh came from below, louder and louder, and a pillar of whiteness rose above the trees, rose and rose, far above where they stood, far above the horizon, gleaming in the light of the low moon, curving over as the mild east wind moved it away.

Again the ground trembled. A huge

boulder, dislodged from somewhere above the cliff, thundered down, leaped over their heads, black against the stars, and went crashing on into the scrub below. From over to their left rose the deep rough grumble of an avalanche, as a whole hillside shifted. Still the ground shook.

Po and Mana huddled against Suth's legs. Noli was quiet again, deep in her trance. Tinu held Otan, merely whimpering. Suth took him. His mind was made up. This was the chance he'd been waiting for.

"Bring Noli," he said. "Come, Mana. Come, Po. We go."

Without waiting for anyone else, he led the way across the moonlit slope. To their left another great column of whiteness soared out of the lake. A warm gust, like a vast moist breath, flowed up the slope. Farther off, with an immense coughing roar, dark orange flames spouted among the trees, with great black lumps hurling up and falling aside, and smaller fiery ones shooting out beyond.

Then it fell quiet for a while. Suth heard the calls and cries of the people scurrying in the other direction toward the nearest place where they could climb the cliff. He ignored them and led the way steadily on toward Tinu's food store.

They were halfway when there was another roar, another uprush of flame from beyond the forest, and the ground shook again, more violently than they'd ever felt it before. Rocks clattered down the slope around them.

They waited, tense, till the tremor ceased, and then hurried on. The food store, when they reached it, had collapsed, but the food was safe beneath the pile. Suth gave Mana and Po a couple of lizards each. He draped the snake and one braid of seed bags around his neck, put the other around Noli's, who seemed to be still in her dream state, and gave Tinu a sheaf of unhusked seed heads to carry in her free hand. He shifted Otan onto his other hip and started to climb, using his digging stick as a staff. Po and Mana scrambled behind, and Tinu led Noli at the rear. The hill did not stir.

After several moons of good food, Otan was a lot heavier than when they had carried him across the Dry Hills, and before long Suth was panting with the effort. He could hear Po and Mana gasping too, and since all seemed quiet he paused to give them a rest. Turning to look back, he saw that the plumes of steam from the lake had drifted away and not renewed themselves, and the two outbursts of fire had steadied to glowing patches, with black smoke churning skyward under the setting moon.

But before they had begun to get their breath Noli, who had been lagging behind while Tinu dragged her on, broke abruptly out of her trance.

"Up!" she cried in her ordinary voice. "Quick, Suth! It is coming!"

She snatched Otan from him and pushed past. He picked Mana up, told Po to grab the other end of his stick, and scrambled after her as fast as his legs would take him until his lungs were retching for air and the blood thundered in his ears.

Through the roaring he heard Po cry out as he lost his hold on the stick and fell. Gasping, Suth turned to wait for him. That was how he saw the first of the major eruptions.

It began with another immense jet of steam from the lake. Before the sound of it reached him, the hillside where he stood leaped, as if it had been struck a blow from beneath, and at the same moment, the whole of the bottom of the valley split open like a bursting seedpod as out from under it rose a boiling orange wave. The roar of its uprush reached him as a blast of scorching wind swept up the slope, knocking him flat.

He rose instantly, dropped his stick, grabbed Po by the arm and dragged him on. Vast burning clods started to fall around them. They'd never make it to the top. He turned aside and headed for a cluster of large boulders, pushed Po and Mana down against the upper side of the nearest one, and lay down above them, shielding them as best he could with his body. A few moments later Tinu was cowering against the next boulder beyond him. He didn't know what had happened to Noli and Otan.

Oldtale
Niglu

Children were born to the daughters of An and Ammu. First born was the son of Nal and of Turka, who were Moonhawk. Thus Moonhawk is first among the Kins, and the other Kins are liars who say that it was among them that the first child was born. They came after.

And they grew to be men and women, and chose mates according to the custom established at Sometimes River, and had children in their turn. So began the Kins.

Then Da and Datta said, "This is not good. You who have mates and children have tens and tens of mouths, and tens and tens of stomachs. You hunt all the game and you pick all the berries and you dig all the roots. There are none left when we come by. There are you eight Kins, and there are us, Da and Datta. That is nine in all. Let the game and the berries and the roots be shared by nines, as it was when we first came to these Places. Then we find our share when we come by."

The others said, "This is not good. You have only two mouths and two stomachs. You cannot eat all of a ninth share. Must our children's children starve, and you two have more than you can eat?"

Da and Datta said, "It must be as we say, as you swore at Odutu below the Mountain."

The others were angry, but they had sworn, so they agreed.

Now, the Kin of Little Bat were at Sometimes River, and Niglu was there. She was the mate of Dag.

Niglu gave birth to a girl baby and took her to a pool of the river to wash clean. But there was thunder and great rain, and the riverbed was filled and they were carried away.

Then Little Bat came flying swiftly and pushed them onto a mudbank near the Gully whose Name is not Spoken.

Niglu came to the gully and saw a garri bush that had been stripped of its berries, all but the share that was Datta's and Da's. And she was very hungry.

She said in her heart, "These are for Da and Datta, but my stomach is empty and I must fill it, or I will have no milk for my daughter."

So she took the berries and ate them, and when her stomach was full she lay down with her baby and slept.

In the evening Da and Datta came to that place, and saw the bush stripped of its berries, and Niglu lying beside it with the juice of the berries on her lips, and they were very angry. In their rage they picked up two rocks and flung them at Niglu and struck her on the temple, so that she died, but the baby lived.

Datta said, "We cannot kill the baby also. I will take it for mine, for I have none."

So they took the child and journeyed by night to Tarutu Rock, and there they hid. For they were afraid for what they had done.

But Little Bat was watching all that happened, and she plucked hairs from Niglu's head and followed Da and Datta, flying very silently. And all along the way she hung the hairs from bushes and trees as she passed.

The next day Dag, who was Niglu's mate, was searching for her along the banks of Sometimes River, and when he came to the Gully whose Name is not Spoken he saw her body lying beside the garri bush. But the child was gone. Then he searched along the gully for the child and came to a tree with a thread of hair hanging from it, and there was blood on the hair, so he knew it for Niglu's.

And a little farther on he found another. Thus he followed the trail that Little Bat had left all the way to Tarutu Rock. There he waited, and in the evening he saw Da and Datta coming down to drink at the dew trap, and with them they had his child.

Dag was very angry, but they were two and he was one, so he went swiftly to his own Kin, who were Little Bat, and to

Snake, which was the Kin of Niglu's father Ral, and told them what he had seen. And they journeyed, all of them, to Tarutu Rock.

In the morning Da and Datta went down to drink at the dew trap, and the Kins of Snake and Little Bat came to them quietly and stood around them and said, "What is this that you did? You killed our Kin and the daughter of our Kin, and you must die."

Da and Datta said, "It was our right. She ate the berries of a garri bush that were our share, according to the oath that you swore at Odutu below the Mountain. How else is one punished who breaks that oath?"

To that they had no answer.

But Dag said, "You killed my mate for a handful of berries. For this I now hunt and kill you, oath or no oath."

So also said Niglu's father, Ral.

But the rest held them fast, and said to Da and Datta, "Go far and far. These we hold for a day and a night and a day. Then we set them free, to do as they choose."

Da and Datta said, "Let it be so. Now we go back to that First Good Place, where we were born. There we hunt and forage and forget you."

So they went, and though Dag and Ral tracked them far and far into the desert, they did not find them, and they were not seen again.

12

The firestorm went on and on. The moon set, but the heavy glare still filled the valley. When Suth raised his head, he could see all along the ridge until the churning column of smoke blanked out the view. Reeking gases fouled the air.

Beside him Mana yelped with pain, then tried to stifle her weeping. A scorching ember had fallen on her arm. Suth licked the place for her and comforted her as best he could, until a fresh rush of gases made him gag and try to throw up.

At last there came a lull in the thundering explosions. Suth rose. Dawn was breaking behind him, graying that half of the sky, but the half ahead of him was black with swirling smoke, rising and spreading as far as he could see, as the wind from the desert pushed it westward.

It was the wind that had saved them. Nothing on the other side of the valley could have lived.

Mana sat up. One whole side of her body was gray with the film of ash that had fallen on her, despite the saving wind. It was the same with Po. Suth looked down and saw that he too was half gray, as if he had been smeared with paste for his man-making at Odutu below the Mountain.

"Noli!" he called. "Noli!"

She rose from behind a boulder a little farther up the slope.

"I live," she called in her normal voice. "I am burned on my leg. Otan lives."

"Wait," said Suth. "I find my digging stick."

The moment he stepped from behind the shelter of the boulder, the heat of the molten lava below swept up at him, hotter than the sun in a desert noon. He could see his stick a little way off, jutting up across the rock on which it had fallen. Otherwise he might not have found it under the layer of ash. Crossing the slope to fetch it, he realized that the dried snake and the braid of seed bags were no longer around his shoulders. He could remember slipping the braid free once they were safely in shelter, but not the snake. Perhaps it had slid off earlier, in the scramble. He was fairly sure he'd still had it when Po had fallen.

He reached the stick, knocked the ash off it, poked around without much hope, found a dried lizard and then, to his great relief, the snake.

He picked them up and carried them back to the others.

"What food do we have?" he said.

His braid of seed bags was by the boulder where he had lain. Tinu had her small sheaf, and Po had clung obstinately to his lizards throughout everything. Mana had dropped both hers, though Suth had found one. He looked at Noli and saw that she had her seed bags intact, but she seemed not to have heard his question.

She was staring at the appalling pillar of smoke. Suth thought perhaps she had gone into one of her trances, but she spoke in her ordinary voice.

"They are gone," she said quietly. "All the old Good Places are gone. Stinkwater and Sometimes River and the dew trap at Tarutu Rock. Gone. Gray stuff buries them, deep, deep. I slept. Moonhawk came. She showed me this."

Suth bowed his head and stood silent. He had no doubt that what she told him was true. *One day I weep for this*, he thought. *One day I tell my own children about the old Good Places. Then they are not forgotten.*

The ground shook. The pillar of smoke convulsed from its base. Huge rocks, golden and orange like the embers of a great fire, flung themselves from it. An immense coughing roar boomed up the slope, followed by another wave of roasting gases.

Suth turned.

"Come quick," he said. "It is not finished."

He took Mana's hand, made Po hang on to his digging stick as before, and hurried them slantwise up the slope, aiming for the gap in the barrier of boulders that he had marked earlier. Gasping, they made their way through it, and rested at last in the shelter on the farther side. Suth passed one of the lizards around, and they took turns chewing, dry mouthed, at the tough and stringy meat.

Suth studied the downward slope. The crack by which they had first climbed the cliff must be almost directly below this point. It would take them all morning, at least, to make their way down it, but at the bottom there was water, and they had food for several days, if they were careful.

He raised his eyes and looked at the desert, already glaring with heat under the risen sun. A dreadful, lifeless place, but he was not afraid of it any more. Cautious, yes, wary, yes, but no longer scared. They could do it. The small ones were strong. They had fed well for many moons.

They would rest by day in the shade of some large rock, moving around it as the sun moved, and in the evening they would set out again. They would find water because it must be there, and Moonhawk would show Noli where to look for it, or else they would find the trail left by those others who had crossed the desert.

And when they had drunk, they would

move on. They would walk and walk under the stars, walk as they knew how to, walk as they were born to, because they were of the Kin. And in the new Good Places beyond the desert they would find the others, and Moonhawk would be Moonhawk once more.

The mountain shuddered. Bits of the crest detached themselves and rumbled away down the slope. The boom of another immense eruption shook the air. The sound seemed to speak to Suth, to tell him that everything that had so far happened was now over and done with, and this dazzling morning was a new beginning.

He rose unhurriedly to his feet.

"Good," he said. "Now it is time to go."